THE NEW DEPUTY

Judge Parker looked at Justin. "I think he'll do, Marshal."

Outside, Justin was light-headed with relief. "I want to thank you, Marshal Yoes."

"That's all right. We needed you."

Sam Dark seemed disappointed. "Button, don't you know why they're so glad to see you; why they need you so much?"

"They're short-handed."

"But don't you know why they're short-handed?"

Justin shook his head. Dark said, "You hear a lot of talk about how many men Judge Parker has sent to the rope, but you don't hear much about how many deputies he's lost bringin' them men in. For every five men the judge has hanged he's lost four deputies killed in the line of duty. Almost one for one.

"You think about that for a while, and then you figure out if I done you a favor."

Bantam Books by Elmer Kelton
Ask your bookseller for the books you have
  missed

HANGING JUDGE
HORSEHEAD CROSSING
LLANO RIVER
MANHUNTERS
THE MAN WHO RODE MIDNIGHT
WAGONTONGUE

HANGING JUDGE

Elmer Kelton

BANTAM BOOKS
TORONTO · NEW YORK · LONDON · SYDNEY · AUCKLAND

*This edition contains the complete text
of the original hardcover edition.*
NOT ONE WORD HAS BEEN OMITTED.

HANGING JUDGE

*A Bantam Book / published by arrangement with
the author*

PRINTING HISTORY

*Bantam edition / January 1984
2nd printing . . . December 1988*

ISBN 0-553-27620-4

Published simultaneously in the United States and Canada

---

*Bantam Books are published by Bantam Books, a division of Bantam Doubleday
Dell Publishing Group, Inc. Its trademark, consisting of the words "Bantam
Books" and the portrayal of a rooster, is Registered in U.S. Patent and
Trademark Office and in other countries. Marca Registrada. Bantam Books,
666 Fifth Avenue, New York, New York 10103.*

PRINTED IN THE UNITED STATES OF AMERICA

O   11 10 9 8 7 6 5 4 3 2

Judge Isaac C. Parker is sometimes portrayed as a ruthless and fanatic hangman, which is an injustice to a well-meaning, dedicated man. When he took over Fort Smith's federal court bench in 1875, Indian Territory was a haven for outlaws, from Texas gunfighters on the dodge to past, present, and future members of the James-Younger-Dalton-Doolin bands, not to mention miscellaneous whiskey runners, horse thieves, bank robbers, and assorted malefactors of every degree. The various Indian nations had their own tribal courts, but these exerted little power over non-Indian lawbreakers.

Like the rider who got the mule's attention by bringing it to its knees with a hickory club, Parker got the attention of the lawless his first year by dropping six murderers through the trapdoor of the big Fort Smith gallows, all at one time. A howl of protest went up in other parts of the country, but not in and around Indian Territory, where honest folk knew the true nature of the enemy.

Early in his career Parker appointed two hundred deputy marshals, whose duty it was to keep peace—or restore it—over 74,000 square miles of Indian Territory. The only other lawkeepers were the Indian tribes' own Lighthorse police. Parker respected Indian law and left to the tribes those affairs which had to do only with Indians. But if a non-Indian was involved, either as culprit or victim, Parker took jurisdiction.

Tragically, Parker is remembered mostly for his hangings. Critics overlook the fact that his rough justice was a product of and perhaps a necessity for the times. He sent seventy-nine men to the gallows during his twenty-one years on the bench. During that time, sixty-five of his deputies were killed in the line of duty. The death toll among the lawbringers was almost as high as among the lawbreakers, at least those who died on the gallows.

The hangings seem less ominous when it is considered that during his hardworking career, he tried more than nine thousand defendants—more than four hundred a year—three hundred forty-four of them for capital offenses. He sentenced one hundred sixty to death, but half escaped the final penalty for one reason or another. None of those seventy-nine who actually walked up the thirteen steps to eternity was convicted for singing too loudly in church. They were a desperate lot, and the times called for desperate measures.

Parker believed in object lessons, which is one reason why he staged several of his gallows "spectaculars," multiple hangings of four to six men at one time. Whatever effect these events may have had on the outlaw element, they managed finally to cause a public outcry and a curbing of Parker's powers. Finally, in 1896, his court was eliminated. By then Parker was already a sick man, and the loss of his bench took the heart out of him. He died two months later.

To the end, the judge maintained that public sympathy was too often misplaced. "Sympathy should not be reserved for the criminal," he declared. "I believe in standing on the right side of the innocent, quiet, peaceful, law-abiding citizen. Is there no sympathy for him?"

George Maledon, Parker's official hangman, saw his own job in a stern perspective. Asked once if any of his victims ever returned to haunt him, he coolly replied that when he sent them away, they never came back.

HANGING
JUDGE

I

Hanging day always drew a crowd to Fort Smith.

Sam Dark had often pondered—without finding answers—the macabre side of human nature that made people travel long miles to watch a man die. If it weren't his job, *he* wouldn't be here. But he was a federal deputy marshal, assigned to keep watch on the people till the trap was sprung, to be on the lookout for any rescue effort or other disturbance. If he had been inclined to gauge crowds with a showman's eye, he would have said Barney Tankard was not a strong draw. Far larger crowds had gathered here on other occasions. Barney Tankard was just one man. The biggest crowds came to witness Judge Isaac Parker's spectacular multiple hangings, when they could see several men drop into Eternity together. Barney Tankard was not even a notable criminal. He was simply a farmer's son who had shot a friend in a drunken quarrel over a half bottle of contraband whiskey. Folks said it was the Indian half of him that made him unable to hold his liquor and the white half that made him pull the trigger. He wasn't basically a bad man, just the wrong man to get drunk.

Sam Dark had been the officer dispatched across the Arkansas River into Indian Territory to fetch Barney for trial. Barney hadn't been wolf enough to get away, for he had never gone afoul of the law before. Catching him had been easy. This was the hard part, to stand here now watching the grim preparations on Judge Parker's big white-painted gallows.

1

Somebody was hawking lemonade at the edge of the milling crowd, catching his dollar wherever it might chance to fall. Dark angered, for it seemed to him a man ought to be allowed some dignity in which to die. Damn it, this wasn't a horse race or a summer picnic. He heard a child shout boisterously and another answer. He glanced around without patience, wanting to send them on their way. Buttons like that . . . they ought to be in school instead of out here waiting to see a man choke to death at the end of a rope . . . but this was hard country and these were harsh times . . . violence so common it was expected like the ague . . . temptation at every fork in the road. Lots of people figured that to see a hanging was part of a boy's proper education, an object lesson in what happens when one allows his feet to stray from the paths of righteousness and into the devious byways of iniquity. This was a thing to make a boy pause and tremble when tempted by an urge to steal a neighbor's ear-corn or to sneak a ride on somebody's mule, the first fateful steps on the well-marked road to the gallows.

Dark surveyed the crowd and found among them a lot of good people—farmers, businessmen, riverfolk—and wondered what the hell they were doing here. A scattering of Indians watched placidly, people come over from beyond Arkansas to see a brother pay for breaking white man's law. If the crime had not been perpetrated against a white man Barney Tankard could have stood trial in tribal courts, for being half Cherokee qualified him as Indian. But it would have made no difference in the final outcome; even the tribal councils decreed death sentences for murder. An Indian convicted in tribal court might be given time to go home and straighten out his affairs, but the end was inevitable. It was a point of honor that upon the appointed day he would appear on his own volition before the council to meet his death like a man, in strength and in dignity. For Barney Tankard there was to be no dignity.

Dark saw a cluster of crib girls, gathered from down on the river, and a couple of them were weeping. He doubted they had ever seen Barney Tankard before. Perceiving little sympathy anywhere else, Dark was glad Barney received at least this much.

The lank, bearded hangman, George Maledon, guided the leg-ironed Barney Tankard onto the double-hinged trap door, and a hush fell over the crowd. Barney glanced up involuntarily at the rope that Maledon had earlier tested with sandbags to be sure it wouldn't kink. In his hands Maledon held the little black bag that would go over Tankard's head. He waited now for the end of the ritual, for the condemned man to speak his last words.

Dark had seen men pray in their final moments. He had heard others caution the onlookers to beware of mistakes that might lead them up these same fatal steps. He remembered a couple who had gone to Eternity cursing.

Given his chance, Barney Tankard stood in silence, a trembling young man still bewildered by a chain of events whose cause he could but dimly recall. He kept his feet only by great effort. His gaze searched the crowd until it found Sam Dark. Dark felt the despair in the dark Indian eyes and wanted to turn away but could not. Tankard summoned some inner strength to have his short say, and he looked straight at Dark as he said it. "What I done was wrong, that I know. But I've prayed, and I'm easy with the Lord. I didn't get here by myself. Them that sold me the whiskey, them that chained me and brought me to this place—they're as bad in their way as I am in mine. I wonder if *they* are easy with the Lord."

Seeing Barney was through the stern Maledon fitted the noose and the black cap. Methodically he reached for the lever.

Dark jerked his head away and shut his eyes. He had watched the first time; he had never made that mistake again. He flinched at the slam of the heavy doors and the sharp gasp from the crowd packed around him.

God, he thought, *what a wretched way for a man to die!*

When he looked again it was not toward the gallows.

He knew nothing had gone wrong there. George Maledon was a precision craftsman who took satisfaction in a job well done. Dark turned to the ugly red brick courthouse, toward the high windows of Judge Parker's chambers. He could see the dim, portly figure of a man standing in the shadows, watching to see that the sentence was duly carried out as he had pronounced it in that austere courtroom. In a moment the figure disappeared.

Gone to pray now in solitude, Dark knew. *But whose soul does he pray for? Barney's? His own? Or maybe for mine and for the rest of us who've got a dirty job to do?*

Dark was particular not to look toward the gallows again. Though he turned away he could still see in his mind the accusing black eyes of Barney Tankard. There wouldn't be any sleep for Sam Dark tonight, not unless he drank himself to it.

The crib girls were walking away now, a couple of them weeping as if Barney were kin. *Every man ought to have somebody weep for him, even if it's just a girl from down on the river.*

The crowd was breaking up, though many people still stared at the grim white gallows as if hypnotized by the image of Death. There wouldn't be any trouble now; he could go. He pushed his way among the people, wanting away from here.

At the edge of the crowd he heard a youthful voice call: "Mister Dark! Could I talk to you a minute, Mister Dark?"

He didn't look around. "Talk to me tomorrow."

"I'd like to talk to you now."

"Boy, can't you see . . ." Dark turned half angrily, looking for whomever had spoken. He saw a man a little past twenty—fresh-eyed, smooth-faced but sunbrowned, wearing a floppy farmer hat and a loose-fitting homespun shirt probably made for somebody else. Sharply Dark said, "I got a right smart on my mind right now, button. I don't feel like talkin' to nobody. Hunt me up another time."

"I come a long ways."

"You shouldn't of. Right now I just want me a good stiff drink. By myself."

The young man went silent. But as Dark proceeded away from the courthouse toward the gin mills on Garrison Avenue, he sensed the lad was following him. Dark turned abruptly. "Are you kin of Barney Tankard?"

"No, sir."

"Kin of somebody else I've brought in for the judge?"

"No, sir."

"Then what's your grudge?"

"I got no grudge, sir."

"If it ain't a grudge, then I wish you'd leave me the hell alone!"

Dark resumed his walk, pushing on through the crowd. Acquaintances hailed him, but he passed them by. He fixed his gaze stonily on a certain saloon and tried to see nothing else. But his eye was caught by a heavy freight wagon standing in the street and a big man checking the trace chains. Dark stiffened at sight of him, and he rubbed a rough hand across his face.

The big man raised up. His mouth smiled but his eyes were hard. "Howdy, Sam Dark. Good hangin'."

Dark's fists knotted. "I don't expect Barney Tankard enjoyed it much."

"You don't need to look at me thataway. I didn't even know the boy."

"But you got his money in your pocket, Harvey Oates. And I expect now you're gettin' ready to go back across into the Territory and peddle some more of the same bad whiskey to other Indian boys who got no tolerance for it."

Harvey Oates kept his sham of a smile. "You want to look in my wagon? You've done it before and you've never yet found a drop of whiskey."

"Someday I will. I'll drag you to the judge, Harvey."

"You'll never find what ain't there. I'm just an honest freighter, that's all. I take the necessities of life to the poor folks out yonder in the wilderness that can't come and fetch it for theirselves." He dropped the smile. "You're a sad case, Sam Dark. You've got to takin' your job too personal, and that's a dangerous thing. You're just supposed to bring them in; you're not supposed to worry about them."

"Most of them I *don't* worry about, Harvey. And when I bring *you* in I'll get a good night's sleep."

Dark turned away from Harvey Oates and elbowed through the swinging door of the saloon. The moustachioed bartender looked at him questioningly. Dark said, "I'm off duty, John."

"You wouldn't be drinkin' if you wasn't, Sam. You done your duty. I heard them doors drop. First drink's on me; I reckon you got it comin'."

Sam Dark had no dependence upon whiskey. He could go without it for weeks at a time and never miss it. Over in the Territory it was forbidden. But he respected whiskey's preventive and curative powers when used at the proper time and place. This was the time. He downed the glass, coughed, then slammed a coin on the bar. "So you don't lose money on me, John. Fill 'er again." He took the glass, careful not to spill anything, and carried it to a small table to nurse it with time and care.

He heard the bartender ask somebody, "What's for you, young fellow?" The reply was in the same voice he had heard at the edge of the crowd. "Nothin', thanks. Mind if I just set myself down here to wait?"

Dark scowled and flung a question halfway across the room. "What you waitin' for, button?"

"For you, Mister Dark. For you to get in the notion to talk to me."

That'll be a while, Dark thought to himself, looking away but not putting the thought into words. He sipped the whiskey, letting it burn his tongue, his throat, wishing it could also burn his brain and erase that image of those black eyes accusing him from the gallows. Times like this he wished he was still following a plow, his eyes looking past the brown rump of a stout Missouri mule. Times there was no price they could pay a man on a job like this that would be half enough. They paid little enough as it was.

He took a long time with the glass of whiskey, and when it was gone he filled it again. The tension had dulled a little. The black eyes that stared at him were blurred some and didn't cut quite so deep.

The farm boy still sat at a table across the room, patiently waiting. *Why don't he get tired and leave?* Dark asked himself irritably. But something sensed rather than seen told him the boy would wait there as long as Dark did.

Dark waved him over. "All right, button, you make as much noise sittin' there quiet as you'd make hollerin' in my ear. Come on and get it said."

The boy pulled out a chair but didn't sit down until Dark motioned for him to. "You don't know me, do you, Mister Dark?"

"Am I supposed to?"

"You was in kind of a fever at the time, but I thought you might remember."

"What time was that?"

"Time you rode up to our cabin bleedin' where somebody had put a bullet through your arm. It had been a right long while, and you was sufferin'. Small wonder you don't remember."

Dark tried to. He reached through the haze of time and through the foggy memories of more than one wound received in the service of the United States District Court. "Would your name be Moffitt, boy?"

The young farmer nodded, pleased. "Yes, sir. Justin Moffitt."

Dark frowned, trying to bring the mental picture into focus. Young Moffitt was right; Dark had been fevered at the time and the whole thing was more like a dream than an actual experience. "Two years back . . ."

"Three."

"Your old daddy helped me into his house. You was a big gangly button but you helped too. Your ma, she cleaned up the wound and wrapped it and fed me some hot grits and pork."

The young man kept nodding. "Yes, sir, that's how it was. Pa tried to get you to stay a couple days and rest, but you rode out, still feverin'. Pa followed after to be sure you made the settlement. We never did hear if you caught your man."

"Not that one. He got away into the Territory and disappeared. They was good to me, your folks. How *is* your daddy, and your ma?"

"Pa's dead, sir. Feller come by one day last winter and started to steal our mare. On the run for the Territory, I guess. Pa tried to stop him. It wasn't no match." Moffitt looked down.

"Sorry about your daddy. He was a Christian. How's your ma?"

"Still pinin' some after Pa, but she's otherwise all right."

Dark lifted his glass as if in a silent toast. He took another drink. "You said you come to talk to me. What about?"

"I'm needin' employment, Mister Dark. I want you to help me get on as a deputy marshal."

Dark's mouth dropped open. "What the hell for? You-all got a farm. Why would you want to take on a job like this?"

"Farm's small. Ma's got my brothers to help her. I need a job."

"Then get one choppin' cotton or sweepin' saloons or workin' the roads. This ain't no life for a boy off of the farm."

"I judge that *you* come off of the farm once."

Dark flinched. "Button, you're not old enough to know what you want."

"I got old enough the day we buried my pa. And I'm not a button. I'm twenty-two."

"When you're on the downhill side of forty like I am, twenty-two looks like a thumb-suckin' age. I bet you got some wild notion that this job'll help you find the man that killed your pa."

"Not likely. Chances are by now he's gone plumb to Texas, or even on to California. But there's plenty others left, just as bad as him. I want to help fix it so other boys won't have to bury their pa the way I done mine."

"A dream, son, that's what it is. And believe me, it'd turn into a nightmare if you stayed with it long enough. What makes you think I'd even consider helpin' you get a job like mine?"

"Maybe you forgot. Before you left our place you said if ever there come a time any of us needed your help all we had to do was ask you. So here I am, Mister Dark, and I'm askin'."

"Best help I could give would be to send you packin' back to where you come from, and that's what I'm doin'."

"You promised you'd help."

"I *am* helpin', more than you know." Dark turned away from him, trying to dismiss him by showing his back. He sensed that the farmer stayed awhile, disappointed. Dark made up his mind to outwait Justin Moffitt. And presently the young man pushed back his chair. Dark heard the slow tread of Moffitt's feet as he retreated out the door.

"Damned buttons," Dark said finally to the bartender, "they never know when they're well off."

The bartender nodded and refilled Dark's glass. "Pity they ever have to learn. Pity they can't stay young and happy and dumb."

"Some do, till it's too late. Some like Barney Tankard . . ."

The afternoon wore away dismally. Some of the hanging crowd had come in for drinks, downed a few and long since departed. It was dusk when finally Sam decided he'd get up from here and go find something for supper. The crowd hadn't bothered him, though he had sensed that a few were talking about him, pointing him out as a Parker bloodhound who rode the dim trails of the Indian Territory, relentlessly seeking out candidates for Parker's judgment and Maledon's carefully oiled ropes. There was respect in their voices, even a touch of fear. But rarely did Dark find liking. That was a thing a man gave up when he took on the job.

He stepped out the door and paused, surprised to find it was so late. His belly was warm from the whiskey and

the coiled tension had left him. He hadn't realized how
time had slipped away. He turned to walk toward the
shack that he used for sleeping and eating when he
wasn't out on business for the court. It had been years
since he had had a home.

Dark felt the hard pressure of blunt, cold steel against
his neck. A voice fell on his ear, quiet and stern. "Just
you take it slow and natural, Mister Dark. Don't act like
there's nothin' wrong or I'll pull this trigger. We're takin'
us a little walk down by the river."

Dark's pistol was in his waistband, beneath his coat. It
had as well have been in the shack, for if he tried to draw
it he would be too dead to pull the trigger. "Don't you
get nervous with that weapon," he said. "Just tell me
whichaway you want me to go."

The man moved the pistol down to Dark's ribs, and
Dark glanced around enough to see him. In the bad light
he thought sure he was Barney Tankard. His stomach
went cold. *Damned whiskey,* he thought, *didn't know
I'd drunk so much.* The man had Indian features,
like Barney's, and a steady hand on that pistol. "Keep
lookin' straight ahead, Mister Dark. You'll see me soon
enough."

Dark walked with him, keeping an outward calm,
which wasn't difficult. He realized he ought to be more
excited than he was, and he knew the whiskey had
dulled him. That was a thing he would have to take into
account—that his reflexes were slowed. Anything he did
he'd have to be damned fast about.

Presently they reached the river and walked beneath a
canopy of tall trees into a patch of heavy shadow. There
Dark made out a small spring wagon with a pine box in
it. He saw a gaunt old man—farmer, by the look of him—
and a heavyset Indian woman. A young girl stood by the
wagon and she looked Indian, too—half Indian, anyway.
The old farmer was white, but Dark knew those features.
He had seen them in the face of Barney Tankard. He
glanced again at the young man who had brought him
here. No, it wasn't the whiskey; the man had Barney's

look. These people would be Barney's family; his father and mother, his sister, his brother.

Dark was sober now. That cold feeling lay heavy in his stomach. "Mister Tankard?" he asked, knowing.

The farmer nodded. "Elijah Tankard. The boy with the gun, that's my son Matthew. The girl is Naomi. And this lady is Barney's mother, Dawn. Cherokee. Good people, the Cherokees."

Dark nodded. He'd known a lot of the Cherokees. "Yes, sir, good people. Mister Tankard, don't you think you ought to be takin' Barney home?"

"In God's due time we'll take him home." The old man's voice was deep and sad. "But we got a family debt that has got to be paid. Always taught my boys . . . a good man pays his debts."

"It'll be a mistake. You'll come to grief."

"Grief? Mister, we already come to grief. Just you look into the face of that boy's mother. She's been singin' a death song. Don't you think we know all there is to know about grief? He was a good boy, our Barney. He didn't go to do nobody any harm."

"He killed a man."

"Wasn't him that done it; it was that rotgut whiskey one of your Fort Smith peddlers sold him. It's them peddlers you ought to be hangin', sellin' that poison to good young Indian boys."

"He didn't have to buy it, Mister Tankard. He didn't have to drink it."

"A boy like that, he don't know. He don't understand the consequences. You forbid a thing and you make it look good to him. If Parker wants to clean up the Territory let him hang the whiskey peddlers that bring the ruin on these people."

"The judge does the best he can. He's sent many a peddler up the river."

"And let as many others get away. He can't hang a man for sellin' whiskey. Leastways he *don't*. And seems like if he can't hang a man he ain't very interested. That rope has gotten to be some kind of a religion with him. He gets drunk on it the way other men get drunk on whiskey."

Dark knew this was an unfair indictment; he also knew he wasn't in a position to argue about it. Far and wide, Isaac Parker was known now as "the hanging judge." He hanged them wholesale sometimes, by twos and threes and even by half dozens. Yet for every man he hanged, Judge Parker sentenced fifty to prison. It was human nature for people to forget about the fifty and remember only the one, and to call Parker a fanatic. "You had me brought out here at the point of a gun, Mister Tankard. That's a prison offense. But I'll forget it if you'll just take that poor boy home and not leave him layin' there on that wagon. He's due some respect."

The girl spoke. At another time and under other circumstances Dark might have looked at her as an individual, might have noticed whether she was pretty or not, whether her voice had a pleasant ring or an ugly one. But his only thought now was that she was an Indian woman, and that Indian men were known, among the wild tribes west, to turn their captives over to the women because the women could be the cruelest ones.

She said bitterly: "Don't you talk about respect for Barney. You brought him here tremblin' for that pious old hypocrite to hang. Barney done just one wrong thing in his life, and that wasn't really his fault. He killed one man. How many have *you* killed, fetchin' them in here like beeves to slaughter?"

Dark looked at the dangerous face of Barney Tankard's brother. He could tell this line of talk was bringing him close to whatever it was they had planned for him. To the father he said, "You better think, Mister Tankard. You already lost one boy. Kill me and there'll be a dozen deputy marshals out lookin' for you. You don't want to stand in front of Judge Parker. You sure don't want this other boy of yours to either. It'd be a pitiful waste."

The old farmer squared his gaunt shoulders. "We wasn't figurin' on killin' you, Sam Dark. But we do intend to fix it so you don't forget the Tankards. To the last day you live you'll remember us."

Dark saw the movement of Matthew Tankard's hand and thrust himself away, trying to escape the clubbing barrel of that six-gun. It struck him a glancing blow that sent his hat spinning and dropped Sam Dark to his knees. A fist—he didn't see whose—slammed into his face and sent wild colors spinning in his brain. The back of his head struck earth.

Fighting to find his balance and push to his feet, he expected another blow. It didn't come. A young voice spoke taut and steely, "Step away from him. I'll shoot whoever makes the next move at him!"

Dark knew the voice. "Don't kill anybody, boy. Let them be."

"Looky what they done to you, Mister Dark."

"Let them be." Dark struggled to his feet, breathing hard. He tasted blood and ran his hand across his mouth, through his moustache. "They done it for cause. Leastways they thought they had cause. Don't shoot anybody, boy. One dead man today is enough."

Justin Moffitt stared hard at the Tankards, not comprehending until his gaze touched the pine box. Realization came into his eyes. "You-all would be Tankards, wouldn't you? From across the river."

The old farmer and his son stood off balance in mute frustration. The girl finally said, "We're Tankards."

For a moment Moffitt appeared to soften, but he looked again at Sam Dark and his mouth went hard. "Then you better be crossin' over. It's been a sad day. Let's don't make it no sadder."

"Boy," said the farmer, "you one of them marshals?"

Moffitt shook his head. The old man said, "Then you butted in where you didn't have no call. There's times when a man ought to just keep walkin' and not see nothin'."

"I got good eyes, Mister Tankard. Sorry about your boy. But Sam Dark here, he just done his job."

The men stared at each other a long time until the older woman said something in a low voice. When she got no response the girl said, "Come on, Papa. We better take Barney home."

Sam Dark still swayed. "Mister Tankard, I meant what I told you—I'm sorry. And I pledge you one thing: I'll do all I can about them whiskey peddlers. They helped your boy fire that gun. I may be callin' on you for help."

Matthew Tankard took a step forward. "You ever show your face at our farm and I'm liable to kill you, Dark!"

The father firmly placed his hand on his son's shoulder. "Ease up, Matthew, you don't mean that. You growed up Christian." To Sam Dark he said, "Right now, tonight, I feel like Matthew does. Maybe in time I'll learn to feel different. If there comes a day when you need help agin them peddlers, and you feel like takin' a chance, you might come by. Maybe we'll shoot you and maybe we won't. Right now I wouldn't make you no promises."

The Indian woman sat on the wagon seat, her head down in silent grief. The girl climbed up beside her, and the old man followed the girl. His eyes hating, Matthew Tankard climbed into the wagonbed beside the coffin. Dark and Moffitt watched them until the night covered them up and only the creak of the wagon wheels indicated the way they had gone. Dark turned to the young man, who still held a pistol in his hand, his arm hanging straight. "You got that thing cocked? You'll shoot yourself in the foot."

His tone was one of mild reproach and Moffitt flared momentarily, having expected gratitude. "I know how to handle a gun."

"If they'd called your bluff what would you have done?"

"I wasn't bluffin'."

Dark decided he wasn't. This young man was serious enough to have shot somebody. "Well, then, I reckon you got me at a disadvantage. You got me owin' you. That's somethin' I don't like to do, is owe somebody."

"You owe me twice," Moffitt pointed out evenly. "Once for tonight, and once for the favor my pa and ma done you."

"And I reckon you'll dog my steps till I pay you?"

"That's exactly what I'll do."

"What'll it take for me to get rid of you?"

"Get me a job as a deputy like I asked you to."

"So people can hate you the way that family hates me? So they'll do to you what these folks almost done to me tonight?"

"Doin' the right thing ain't always popular. But it's always right."

Dark frowned. "First you got to always be sure what *is* right. Half the time nowadays I can't make up my mind." He shrugged finally. "I can't promise you a job, but I do promise you we'll talk about it. Where you stayin' at?"

"Noplace. Anyplace. I got a blanket on my saddle and a warbag with a little grub in it. I just sleep where night catches me."

"Well tonight it's caught you in Fort Smith. I got me a shack down here a ways. Only one bed and that's mine. But you can spread your blanket on the floor if you're a mind to."

"I'd be tickled, Mister Dark."

Dark turned and started to walk. In a minute he stopped. "I never did tell you thanks. I reckon I ought to." He sounded almost grudging.

"Get me a job, and that'll be thanks enough."

"Maybe. And then again maybe the day'll come that you'll wish you'd passed on by and let the Tankards do what they had in mind."

II

Justin Moffitt didn't sleep well. It wasn't the hard plank floor that bothered him; he could sleep on a floor or even the bare ground about as easily as on the best corn-shuck mattress in some nice hotel that changed the bedclothes every week. Most of the night he lay trying to frame the arguments he would use on Sam Dark in the morning. He sorted out all the facts and put them up in one-two-three order, like drygoods on a shelf, and knew that when the time came to talk they would tumble out ingloriously, leaving him struggling for words. Justin Moffitt had always been handy with tools—an axe, a knife, a saw. He'd always been an easy learner with guns, whether a pistol or an old muzzleloading squirrel rifle like the one his granddaddy had fetched down from the hills of Tennessee. With those things Justin Moffitt was in his element. But with words he was next to helpless. He couldn't argue or plead a case.

"You'll turn out to be a good farmer and not much else," his father had told him. "There's nothin' to be ashamed of in that. You seldom see a rich farmer but you seldom see a hungry one, either. Long's he can grow a little somethin' to eat they can do their damndest against him and never quite starve him to death."

Maybe he *would* end up a farmer; Justin had no dread of the life. In fact he sort of liked it. But first he wanted at least to try for something that might be better.

Ever since they had moved into the big country near the Arkansas Justin Moffitt had been aware of the criminal element that constantly drifted through, much of it on the way to the vast obscurity that was the Indian Territory. He had been aware of his father's hatred for the type who dropped by isolated farmhouses and demanded food and horse feed as a divine right, a kind of forced tribute in return for leaving farmer and family unhurt. Like others of their kind, the Moffitts suffered these indignities because of the awesome price for fighting back individually. They observed the code of silence when lawmen came around, for lawmen never stayed long and the lawless were never far away. They sometimes exacted a terrible price from those who gave information.

Justin's father had stayed because he had faith that law would come here as it had come elsewhere and the land was rich with promise. "All we got to do," he said, "is hold tight and outlive the outlaw."

Justin had seen lawmen who seemed more inclined to avoid the criminals than to find them. Some, he thought, were little better than criminals themselves. One day Sam Dark had ridden up to the Moffitt farm, wounded and in need of help. He had accepted what treatment was necessary, then had ridden on doggedly in search of his assailant. This was a kind of man Justin Moffitt had never seen before. This was the kind of man he made up his mind he wanted to be. It was a tenet of the Moffitt family faith that a man owed a debt to his country and to the people who gave him life; he owed it to them to try to make the country better than it was. After meeting Sam Dark, Justin Moffitt thought he knew where his duty lay, how his debt was to be paid. When his father died, brutally murdered by a passing horse thief, Justin knew for sure.

He lay awake as daylight slowly penetrated the shack, bringing detail to the vague forms he had looked at through the night—a bare wooden table, two rawhide chairs, a small cast-iron stove with a stack of red bricks substituting for one lost leg. A lank, striped tomcat stretched idly under the edge of Sam Dark's cot, eyeing Justin distrustfully as an intruder, upsetting the accustomed order of his small kingdom. Sam Dark had slept fitfully, talking occasionally to Barney Tankard. Now he turned, causing the cat to rise up expectantly. Dark's eyes came open. He blinked a moment, then looked balefully at Justin lying on the floor, as if he had hoped Justin would lose heart and slip out during the night, leaving him alone.

His voice was gritty. "If you want any breakfast, button, you'll have to go out and chop some wood."

Justin flung his blanket aside. He had slept in his clothes—all but his shoes. He laced them hurriedly. When he returned with an armload of wood he found Dark had most of his clothes on and was fanning flame into some kindling. Dark took a little of the wood and motioned for Justin to drop the rest into a box. "Ain't much to eat around here. Coffee . . . sidemeat . . . biscuits." Dark ground some coffee beans and poured them into a pot. He walked over to the cabinet and picked up a wooden bucket, then turned impatiently. "If the damned shack was to catch on fire, first thing to burn would be the water bucket." He thrust it at Justin. "Cistern's at the corner of the house."

There wasn't room for two to work so Justin stood back and watched Dark pinch pieces of sourdough from a batch kept in a crock jar. The house was a boar's nest and in need of sweeping, but Justin figured he would raise dust and send Dark into a fit of irritation. He needed Dark on his side, not against him.

He silently studied the graying deputy, feeling that here was an uncommon man and wondering if he could somehow observe what it was that made him that way. He saw nothing evident in Dark's face to set him apart. Dark was well into middle age, creases cutting around the edges of his eyes, down past his moustache, under his stern jaw and down the stubble of his neck. His hide was brown as any farmer's. In fact he would pass anywhere for a farmer were it not for something indefinable in his manner, something in the way he carried himself and in the watchful seriousness of his gray eyes.

Justin's father had once told him, "It's hard for a good lawman to slip into a town and not be noticed. He betrays himself by the way he walks, the way he sits a horse, the way he looks at people like he was judgin' them and sortin' the wheat from the chaff. He develops habits he can't put aside. He don't have to wear a badge. It shows on him."

The day Sam Dark had ridden up to the Moffitt farm Justin had instinctively known him for what he was before he ever saw the badge. He never quite understood how.

He wanted to make conversation but he didn't wish to push himself, considering how badly he needed Sam Dark's favor. He waited for Dark to open the talk and Dark seemed in no mood for it. They ate in silence, Dark staring out the open door, eyes pinched, forehead furrowed in concentration.

At length Justin started to drop a strip of the sidemeat to the tomcat on the floor. Dark frowned. "I wouldn't. Never feed him myself. I'm gone too much and he's got to stay used to makin' his own livin'. He'd suffer for it if I was to spoil him." Dark finished his third cup of black coffee before he stood up and walked to the door to pitch the grounds out into the bare yard. "You said you was pretty good with a pistol. Come show me."

Justin's pistol lay on the floor beside his rolled-up blanket. Dark stepped out into the yard, looking around a moment, then pointing. "Yonder's somebody's milk goat with a bell around its neck, stealin' my horsefeed. Let's see if you can hit the bell and not kill the goat."

Seemed like a safe gamble, using somebody else's livestock, and Justin raised the pistol and squeezed the trigger. The little bell exploded. The goat blatted in panic and sprinted away like a startled deer. Justin lowered the smoking pistol. "What else you want me to shoot?"

The shot had stirred a dozen or so dogs into wild barking, and in a house across the road Justin saw a woman and three children rush to the door to see what had happened. Dark shook his head. "Nothin'. Just wanted to see what you could do." He watched impassively as the frightened goat disappeared around a turn in the weed-lined trail. "That goat wasn't fixed to shoot back at you, though. Think you could do as good against a man who was?"

Justin stared at the smoking pistol. "I might not. Never tried."

Dark nodded. "Honest answer. That's in your favor, anyway." He held out his hand for Justin's pistol and Justin handed it to him butt first. Dark turned it over in his big palms, inspecting it critically. "You've slept on everything I told you yesterday. Still got your mind made up?"

"Been that way a long time."

"Then I'll take you to Jacob Yoes. He's the chief U.S. marshal. He'll pass on you first and then most likely take you before Judge Parker. But if Yoes thinks you're all right the judge'll take him at his word."

"And if you think I'm all right will Marshal Yoes take you at your word?"

Dark's brow creased again. "You know you're usin' me, don't you?"

"I'm sorry. I wouldn't do it if I knew any other way."

"Well I gave you my feelin's, and you're of legal age. I won't stand in your way even though I think you're wrong."

"Thanks, Mister Dark."

"Thank me sometime when I've done you a favor."

Jacob Yoes was a preoccupied man with worry in his eyes and frustration in his manner. His desk was piled high with fugitive notices and unserved warrants; with expense claims from the dozens of deputy marshals riding the Territory in search of the lawless, who outnumbered the deputies by scores to one. That was reason enough to turn a man's milk into clabber. Dark introduced Justin, but Yoes showed more interest in the cuts on Dark's face left by the encounter with the Tankards. "What happened to you, Sam?"

"Oh, nothin', sir. Just fell off of a porch."

Yoes gave Justin the same careful, half-suspicious scrutiny Sam Dark had given him. The marshal asked Dark, "Do you vouch for this man?"

Dark said, "He comes from Christian folks. He's showed me he knows how to handle a gun." Justin waited for Dark to relate last night's incident, but he didn't. Dark thought a moment, then added, "That's all I can tell you about him." Justin felt disappointed. Dark probably didn't want to cause trouble for the Tankards, but that story would have impressed Yoes and strengthened Justin's case.

Yoes put his fingertips together and stared over them at Justin. "Young man, do you know how many of this court's deputies have died in the performance of their duties since Judge Parker has presided?" When Justin shook his head the marshal said, "Close to forty. And there'll be more. That's why there are vacancies in my force today. That's why there are almost always vacancies. One mistake, one stroke of bad luck and you could be just another name on this court's long, sad honor roll."

"I don't plan to make no mistakes, sir."

Justin realized instantly that he had sounded braggy. He hadn't meant to. "What I intended to say, sir, is that I'll be careful and I'll do my duty. I owe it to my father."

Whatever doubts he might have harbored, Yoes put them aside. "I see no reason to turn you down, then. But the final authority rests with the judge. We'll go and see him."

Yoes ushered Justin into an upstairs office, trailed by Sam Dark. In a desk by the window, his back half turned to the door, a tall, heavy-set man sat bent over several spread-out law books, the thick forefinger of his right hand laboriously tracing the lines of fine print. His black frock coat was a bit threadbare and there was about the man an air of austere dignity.

"Judge Parker, sir . . ." Yoes spoke with respect and with implied apology for the disturbance, for court was due to convene shortly and the judge seemed to be trying to establish some legal points in his mind. Parker turned slowly and without concern, for he evidently

knew Yoes by his voice. It occurred to Justin that a man
who had made as many enemies as Isaac Parker was
taking a grave risk in leaving his door open and
unguarded. Anyone could walk in here and murder him
in cold blood. God knew there were plenty who might
believe they had reason enough. But it was said the
judge walked the streets of Fort Smith alone and
unarmed, quietly demonstrating that his court would not
be intimidated though it be surrounded by the most
dangerous aggregation of unhung criminals west of the
Mississippi.

For years Justin had heard awed talk of Judge Parker;
he somehow expected to see a vindictive man sitting like
an angry Deity high upon a throne, hurling thunderbolts
down upon the wicked. This man appeared to be
anything but that. On the street Justin would have taken
him for a minister. He was not old, probably not much
more than fifty, for gray was just now beginning to streak
his hair and beard. But to a man of twenty-two, fifty is
old. Parker reached absently for the golden watch chain
that dangled across his broad middle. He glanced at the
time, his eyes blinking in uncertainty because his mind
was still partly upon the lines he had been reading. He
appeared relieved that it was not yet time for court.

This, Justin thought in surprise, could not be the
legendary fanatic, the cruel-eyed hanging judge they
whispered about all over Arkansas and across the
Territory, the man who remorselessly played God with
the lives of those unfortunates brought before him.

Parker saw the marks on Sam Dark's face. "What
happened to you, Mister Dark?"

"Fell off of a horse, your honor."

Yoes blinked, for he had heard a different version.
Parker's eyes shifted to Justin, plainly wondering if he
were some felon hauled up for judgment. Yoes said,
"Judge Parker, this young man is Justin Moffitt. He
wants to join the service of this court as a deputy
marshal."

Parker's blue eyes studied Justin as they might study a

criminal in the dock, searching for some flaw. "Have you examined him, Marshal Yoes? Does he seem qualified?"

"As far as I can tell, your honor."

Judge Parker pushed slowly to his feet, and only then did Justin realize how tall and how large the man really was. He seemed to tower over Justin Moffitt. "You're young, Mister Moffitt, but we've had younger men in the service of this court. That won't weigh against you. What concerns me is your purpose, your reason. Is it money?"

"No, sir. I hear deputy marshals don't make much money."

"True, not from the government at least. But there is more than ample opportunity for a misguided man to use his badge and make money from illicit sources if he is of that type. We've tried to be careful in picking men, but we've made a few mistakes."

"Such a thing never entered my mind, your honor."

"Good. See that it never does, for let me warn you of one thing. This court is thoroughgoing against all the lawless, but it is absolutely merciless with a lawman gone wrong. I'll expend more effort to punish a man of that stripe than any other class of criminal except a murderer. A peace officer carries a degree of trust equal to that borne by a man of God. When he betrays it he forfeits all claim on the generosity of his fellow man."

"I'll be true to your trust, sir."

The judge studied him a moment more with a solemn, searching gaze that made Justin extremely self-conscious about his inexperience, his farmer look. He had an uneasy feeling that Parker could read in his face every little mistake, every petty sin Justin had ever committed. Finally the judge looked at Yoes. "I think he'll do, Marshal Yoes. How many young men today still remember to say 'sir'?"

Justin followed the marshal to the door. The judge called after him, "Mister Moffitt! I didn't ask you, but I take it you're a churchgoing man?"

"Yes, sir, when there's a church available."

"There are several here in Fort Smith. I hope I'll see you in mine."

"You will, sir." Justin would make a point of it.

The judge turned back to his desk. But now, instead of the law books, he picked up a huge, black-bound Bible. He seemed to know just where to open it, and he immersed himself in the reading of the Word.

Walking down the hall with Yoes and Sam Dark, Justin was light-headed with relief. Outdoors he would have whistled, but here he sensed the dignity of the court. He restrained himself. "I want to thank you, Marshal Yoes."

"That's all right. We needed you."

Dark seemed disappointed. "Button, don't you know why they're so glad to see you; why they need you so much?"

"They're short-handed."

"But don't you know why they're short-handed?"

Justin shook his head. Dark said, "Marshal Yoes as good as told you. You hear a lot of talk about how many men Judge Parker has sent to the rope, but you don't hear much about how many deputies he's lost bringin' them men in. For every five men the judge has hanged he's lost four deputies killed in the line of duty. Almost one for one. You think about that a while, and then you figure out if I done you a favor."

III

Marshal Yoes took Justin into his office and explained the details of the job, the routine for claiming expenses, the manner of remuneration. "I'll assign you to one of the more experienced men. Since Sam Dark brought you here I'll let him take the responsibility of breaking you in."

Sam Dark's face creased in silent protest but he didn't give voice to it. He walked to the window and looked out, hiding his dislike for the idea. In a moment he said, "Then, button, we'll start breakin' you in right now. Yonder comes Rice Pegler and the tumbleweed wagon."

Justin wasn't sure he had heard. "The what?"

"The tumbleweed wagon." Dark gave him a quick look of impatience. "Come on, let's go downstairs."

Half suspecting he was being hoaxed, Justin followed. Outside and halfway down the broad stone steps he stopped. A small crowd was rapidly gathering around a long freight wagon. A Negro driver climbed down from the wagon seat. Two armed riders, each carrying a rifle in his lap, moved up on either side. One—a tall, angular deputy whose face was half hidden beneath a broad-brimmed gray hat—motioned sharply to half a dozen men seated in the bed of the wagon. "All right, you good citizens climb out of there and be damn quick about it!"

The men moved stiffly, cramped from riding in an unaccustomed position. They wore leg irons and all were hitched to each other by a long chain.

Dark was on the ground and halfway to the wagon.

Curtly he signaled Justin to come. "You wanted a job. Let's get after it."

The Negro driver walked to one of the horsemen who handed him a pistol. Justin surmised that he drove the wagon unarmed so no prisoner could grab a weapon from him. The Negro strode stiffly toward Sam Dark, smiling. "Howdy, Mister Sam. Glad we found you to home."

Sam Dark shook hands with him. "Howdy, George. Looks like you caught you a fair bunch of them at home this time."

"Fair haul, Mister Sam. But I reckon there ain't none of us as good a fisherman as you." He glanced at the horseman with the flat-brimmed old gray hat as if expecting rebuttal.

The horseman swung a long leg over the horse's rump and dropped easily to the ground. His bestubbled face broke into a hard, ironic grin. There was no humor in it but rather, if anything, a subtle malice. "I'd say we done pretty good, Sam. Even hooked one *you* been lookin' for a long time and never could catch." The tall deputy shifted his gaze back to the wagon. He shouted harshly, "Come on, I said climb out of that wagon! I don't intend to stand here all day!"

One of the prisoners, who appeared to be a half-breed Indian, muttered something under his breath. The words were muddled but the message was clear. The tall man took two steps forward and swung his fist, throwing the full power of his shoulders into it. The prisoner staggered backward and struck his head solidly against the wagon. "Anybody else wants to talk ugly to me I got another dose of the same bitters waitin' for him." His gaze fell distrustfully upon Justin Moffitt. "Who are you? How come you standin' here?"

Dark said, "Rice, he's a new deputy. Judge just hired him."

Rice Pegler eyed Justin half belligerently. "If you're drawin' federal money then get to earnin' it. We got prisoners to take to the cells."

Not sure what he was supposed to do but knowing he had better do something in a hurry, Justin drew his pistol. He moved around the back of the wagon where the last prisoner was awkwardly climbing down, carefully trying to avoid pain to a bandaged arm. Justin felt a little foolish pointing the pistol at the men. He had no real idea what he was doing.

The smiling Negro came to his rescue. "Howdy, boy. You want to help me take these men inside to school? I'll go and open the door. You stay behind them and make sure there don't none of them run off. Them leg irons costs money." He glanced at Justin's pistol. "And if you was to decide to shoot somebody, I sure do hope it ain't me."

His matter-of-fact manner took away much of Justin's uncertainty and his friendliness gave Justin ease. It occurred to him that none of the prisoners could run unless they all did. They were chained together. He hadn't been afraid of them. Rather, he had been afraid of himself; afraid he would make a mistake at the start and look a fool.

The tall deputy made Justin feel like a fool simply by the way he looked at him.

But the deputy didn't watch Justin long. He concentrated on Sam Dark. "You owe me the drinks, Sam. I brung in the man that shot you a couple of years ago. He don't look like much now, does he?"

Sam Dark didn't reply. He stared at the prisoner with the bandaged arm. The deputy was badgering him and Sam Dark was plainly trying not to be graveled by it. Dark finally said, "Don't matter to me who got him long's he's got."

"I'm the one that got him," Pegler stressed.

Justin could tell it did matter to Sam Dark, despite what he said. Dark asked, "How come the bandage on him?"

"I shot him," the deputy replied.

"But why?"

"Why not? If *you'd* shot him when you had a chance to he wouldn't of put a bullet in you. You'd be surprised how a little chunk of lead weighs a man down and keeps his mind off of mischief."

Dark pondered soberly. "Then you must not be the shot you used to be, Rice."

"How's that?"

"You hit him in the arm. You always aim at the heart."

The Negro unlocked the door that led to the jail cells. Rice Pegler and another deputy followed him, then turned to watch the chained prisoners file in. Sam Dark and Justin Moffitt brought up the rear. Justin was keenly aware that a considerable crowd had gathered outside, watching. He felt as if everyone had eyes on him. He decided that was foolish; they were curious about the prisoners.

Inside the jail he heard a cry go up among those men already in confinement. They were greeting the new crop. Some called individuals by name. One shouted, "Break and run! Better they shoot you than throw you in this hellhole!"

Justin had never been in a jail. He had thought he knew what to expect but the foul, choking air caught him by surprise. He took an involuntary step backward, toward the clean outdoors. Sam Dark caught his astonished look and grunted for him to stand his ground. Justin felt as if he would throw up, but he got control. The stench was overpowering. A low ceiling, a stone floor and the small barred windows conspired to trap the smells of human excrement. Slop pails stood partially filled, adding to the problem during the long, hot hours they waited for a guard or trusty to pick them up and empty them. Little fresh air found its way in here, much less circulated. Mopping the stone floors only intensified the problem by soaking down all the spillings and leaving the stone and mortar saturated with them.

The older prisoners were bearded and dirty for washing facilities were limited. Their clothes were filthy, every fiber penetrated by the grime and the stench of the place. Some expressed sympathy for the new prisoners being unshackled one by one and herded through the barred doors of the overcrowded cells. An Indian prisoner stepped up and embraced the half-breed. The new prisoners looked around anxiously among those already here, searching for old friends—or old enemies.

Sam Dark said, "We better get a doctor in here when we can, to look at that man's wound."

Rice Pegler scowled. "He didn't call no doctor to look after yours. If I was you I'd let him sweat. It'll either get well or it'll kill him."

"We'll get him a doctor," Dark repeated.

Pegler stared into the cell, his craggy face contemptuous. "Suit yourself, but I sure as hell ain't goin' to pay for it. Look at them animals there—Indians, niggers, white trash. Far as I'm concerned, they got nothin' comin' but jail or a rope." He watched the last cell door swing shut with a hard clang that must have had an awful finality about it to the men newly locked inside. Glancing once more at Dark he shook his head and walked out muttering about being hungry.

Justin didn't think *he* would ever be hungry again. He waited for Sam Dark to do something or say something. Dark just stood looking through the bars at the wounded prisoner who had shot him a long time ago. Justin finally said, "I expect Pegler's right. If they hadn't done one thing or another to deserve it they wouldn't be here."

Dark didn't look at him. "They're fugitives till I catch them. After that they're men." He turned and left the jail. Justin followed after him, sensing that in agreeing even a little with Rice Pegler he had somehow erred, had not raised himself in Sam Dark's eyes.

Justin found that much of the marshals' and deputies' work was routine. It involved a great deal of paperwork. Watching Rice Pegler laboriously scrawl his way through a lengthy report of his mission with the tumbleweed wagon, Justin wondered how many people would ever eventually read all that writing. The way it appeared to him the federal government was more concerned with getting the papers filled out properly than it was with capturing fugitives. Rice Pegler expressed his view of it: "Way I see it it's all politics, our government is. The party that gets in, it's got to have a lot of jobs to give the

people who worked hard to get it elected. It don't matter
how good they work for the government; it's how they
worked for the party that counts. These people got to
have jobs so they make jobs for them a-readin' all them
reports. No reports, no jobs. No jobs the party don't get
back in come next election. So we write reports when
there's badmen out yonder that needs hangin'."

Of all the deputies Justin found himself on the easiest
terms with the Negro, George Grider. Grider had an
infinite patience in explaining things and there was much
that Justin needed to have explained.

Rice Pegler had a certain crude attraction for Justin
because of his tough, straightforward way of looking at
things. Pegler never bothered himself pondering the
delicate balances between right and wrong. To him each
thing was either one or the other, instantly recognizable,
beyond question. Pegler asked him, "You never did see
the man that shot your daddy, boy? Then how you goin'
to ever know if you come across him?"

Justin confessed that he had no idea.

"The thing to do," Pegler said sternly, "is to figure
them all the same. Figure every criminal might be the
one that killed your daddy. Look at him the way you'd
look at a snake. Don't ever give one of them a halfway
even chance because he's as liable to kill you as to look at
you. When in doubt, shoot. And when you shoot, kill a
man. It's a lot cheaper on the government to do a buryin'
than to put on a trial."

Once he became accustomed to the smell Justin spent
much of his spare time in the jail, quietly looking over
the prisoners until he knew every face. He kept
wondering if one of them just *might* be the man he had
hoped someday to meet. The longer he looked at most of
them the more inclined he was to share Pegler's view.
They were a coarse, hard lot for the most part—rough-
looking, rough-talking, showing no particular remorse
for the crimes they had committed, though many were
fearful of the consequences when once they were
brought before the judge. A number already had had
their day in court and were waiting here for the carrying

out of judgment. It was a short walk out of the cell, down
that corridor, out into the sunlight and up those fateful
steps.

Times, Justin was detailed to help escort prisoners to
court. Usually these men were bathed and shaved and
an effort made to present them in a manner befitting the
dignity and high purpose of the federal court. One
prisoner he guarded was a murderer who had waylaid
and coldly knifed an Indian cowboy for the meager
wages in his pocket. Justin had only contempt for him.
Yet a chill ran down Justin's back as the prisoner stood for
sentencing and Judge Parker's usually benevolent mien
gave way to a fearful vengeance. The judge reviewed the
stark facts of the case, commented upon the cruel nature
of the crime, then set the date of execution and said in a
powerful voice: "I sentence you to hang by the neck until
you are dead, *dead*, DEAD!"

During his confinement the prisoner had made a show
of toughness, often bragging of the defiant statement he
would make to the judge when he had the opportunity to
stand before him in court. Now he stood cowed, face
pale. As Justin helped escort him back down to the
dungeon he noted that the man was wet, and not
altogether from perspiration.

"They can't do that to a man," he whimpered to all
who would listen. "They can't just take a man's life away
from him thataway. It's murder."

It was on Justin's mind to tell him he should have
thought of that before he took another man's life without
any thought to rights. But the cold reality of the death
sentence had never quite reached him before, and Justin
stood in awe of the power concentrated in that huge man
on the judge's bench.

Rice Pegler was in awe of nothing. He told the
prisoner, "Quit your whimperin'. Bible says what ye sow,
that shall ye reap. And you sure planted yourself a crop."

IV

In the first weeks Justin Moffitt worked a lot of long days and nights, but all of them seemed to be in or near Fort Smith. He longed for an assignment that would send him out into that seemingly limitless, mysterious Indian Territory that lay tantalizingly within sight across the river. Other deputies were coming and going all the time, some bringing prisoners for the crowded jail, others telling stirring stories of exciting near-captures. But Marshal Yoes didn't choose to send Justin on these missions. Justin suspected Sam Dark was responsible for keeping him in town. Dark coached him, often curtly; more inclined to tell him of his mistakes than to acknowledge the far greater number of things he did right the first time. Justin continued to stay at Dark's shack, sharing the rent with him, helping buy the grub, but wondering sometimes if he ought to move out. After all he had the job now, and he had learned a lot about the way a deputy went about the performance of his duties.

He worried, when he had stretches of time on his hands, about Dark's attitude. To the sympathetic Negro, George Grider, Justin said, "I don't see no good reason for him to keep a-ridin' me the way he does. I do my job. I don't make too many mistakes."

Grider frowned, offering a nod but no advice. Justin expressed one recurring suspicion, that Dark was a strongly self-reliant man—he had shown that on many occasions—and didn't like to stand beholden to anyone. Perhaps it had offended him that Justin had reminded

32

him of a moral debt owed the Moffitt family. Sam Dark
had resisted help until resistance was futile. Perhaps he
felt less of a man because in the end he had been
dependent upon someone else.

"Sometimes I wish Marshal Yoes had assigned me to a
man like Rice Pegler instead of to Sam Dark," Justin
said.

Grider was surprised. "Rice Pegler?"

"Why not? He sure don't ever back away from nothin'
or nobody, does he?"

Grider pondered a moment and avoided a direct
answer. "He does his job, that Mister Rice."

"I'd like to be able to get along with Sam Dark. But if
he don't want to get along I reckon I don't really need
him anymore. I got the job now. What do you think,
George?"

Not many people spent time with George Grider for
to them his color was wrong. It pleased him that Justin
Moffitt kept seeking him out for news and advice, for
someone to share talk with. He said, "I'd give Mister
Dark more time, if I was you. He don't mean you no
harm."

"Then how come he acts like he does?"

"I think because when he looks at you he sees hisself,
young again, and sometimes he ain't too awful proud of
hisself nomore. Give him time, boy."

One night Justin was awakened by someone knocking
on the frame of the open door. Sam Dark was up from his
cot instantly, pistol in his hand. "Who's out there?"

"I come peaceful," replied a voice far from young.
Justin could see the outline of a gaunt, slightly stooped
man against the moonlight. "I'm Elijah Tankard."

"Tankard?" Dark's voice was incredulous. "You alone,
Mister Tankard?"

"I'm by myself. I come for no harm; I come to help
you . . . and to help me, too."

Dark considered a moment. "All right, Mister Tankard, I'm takin' your word. You come on in."

Justin felt a little foolish, standing there in his
underwear, but Sam Dark was the same way and it didn't

seem to be of the slightest concern to him. Dark said, "I'll light the lamp."

The old farmer put up his hand. "Might be just as well you didn't. I don't know that anybody in town would recognize me, but there ain't no use takin' the risk, is there?"

"Not if you got reason to think there *is* a risk." The way Dark said it he was putting a question to the old man without actually asking it.

Elijah Tankard found a rawhide chair in the reflected light of the moon but he didn't sit in it. He braced his hands and leaned his weight against its straight back. "You got cause to distrust me after what me and my boy Matthew done to you. And I reckon we got cause to hate you for you deliverin' my youngest boy Barney to the hangman. I can't rightly say I feel any kindness toward you, Dark; I doubt as ever I will. But whatever I think of you I hate them whiskey peddlers ten times worse. It was them that put the devil in my boy's mouth. Now they're back in our parts again, lookin' for other boys to ruin with that poison. If you'd like to catch them, Dark, I'll take you ever step of the way."

Dark stood hunched, not over his surprise. "You know they won't hang for peddlin' whiskey. Worst they'll get is time in prison."

"They ought to hang like my boy did. But better a stretch in the pen than out runnin' free and leadin' good boys astray."

Dark peered a moment at Justin Moffitt, then turned his attention back to the farmer. "Mister Tankard, would you mind waitin' outside? I want to talk this over with Deputy Moffitt."

Disappointed, Tankard observed, "You don't believe me."

"I don't *disbelieve* you. But you can see how it'd be if you was in my place; I need to talk to Moffitt."

Tankard nodded and walked out. Justin could hear a horse stamping a foot. Just one horse. He looked.

Dark said, "He sounds honest."

Justin frowned. "He still hates you; he as good as said

so. Could be he's baitin' a trap to snap your head clean off."

"Could be. But I want to believe him, Justin."

"Anyhow, is it worth the risk? Like you said, worst they could give anybody for runnin' whiskey would be a stretch in jail. They sell whiskey here in Fort Smith right across the bar, legal as anything. What makes it so bad when they do the same thing in the Territory?"

"You and me, Justin, we're white. White men been drinkin' that stuff since before God wrote the Bible. We got it in our blood, and we're immune to it, to some extent. But it's new to the Indian. He didn't inherit none of that immunity. He can drink just a little of it and go plumb roarin' crazy, do things he wouldn't ever consider doin' if he was of a sound mind, sell his land, rent his wife, kill a friend the way Barney Tankard did. You'd about as well kill an Indian as to sell him whiskey. Old man Tankard knows that."

"Just the same, I wouldn't trust him no further than I could spit. You ride off with him you just may not ever come back."

"I wasn't figurin' on goin' with him alone."

Moffitt's eyes widened. "You takin' me into the Territory?"

"You been faunchin' around here like a stud colt, wantin' to get out yonder. Maybe now we'll find out if you can really earn your keep."

"I can take care of myself."

"I'm more interested in whether you can help take care of *me!*" Still standing in his underwear, Dark put on his hat and then began reaching for the rest of his clothes. "We'll have to go report to Marshal Yoes. We'll get old black George to follow after us in the tumbleweed wagon, holdin' back a day or so to keep from flushin' the game before we're ready."

Justin began to tingle. "Rice Pegler's in town. Maybe we ought to get him to go with us."

Dark looked at him in sharp disapproval. "Not Rice Pegler. We can do it, you and me. And if you can't do it, then I'll do it myself—*by* myself."

"We can do it, Mister Dark."

"Then I want you to remember one thing: you'll do what I tell you. Don't hold back and don't ask no damn fool questions. Agreed?'

"Agreed."

It took them a couple of hours to get the legal necessities taken care of and proper directions given to the Negro. Elijah Tankard waited at Dark's shack, out of sight.

"It ain't like I was afraid of anybody," he explained later, after they had crossed the river and set their horses upon the trail west. "But there's folks in Fort Smith that know me. If they seen me with you they might figure out what I was up to and send word ahead of us. Especially a man like Harvey Oates."

The name meant nothing to Justin, but he saw Sam Dark come to attention. "What about Harvey Oates?"

"You know as well as I do; it's common knowledge in the Territory that he supplies most of them whiskey peddlers. Them freight wagons of his are just to hide his real trade."

"His wagons've been searched. I've done it myself many a time. Nobody's ever found anything that wasn't supposed to be there."

"And you ain't apt to. There ain't enough marshals in the whole United States to check everything that comes into the Territory."

"One of these days we'll catch him."

"I'd love to be there."

They rode all day across green hills and wooded lowlands, past clear-running creeks and through long, lush valleys that had never felt the bite of the plow. This was yet Territory land, officially reserved for the Indian, though, through marriage to Indian women or with maneuvering of many types of available permits, it was home now to as many white men as red. Farm-raised Justin could tell by the look of it that this country was ripe for the picking, the flatlands fairly begging for the bull-tongue plow, the rolling grasslands waiting for the white man's herds. A good many cattle already were scattered upon it, some probably having no right to be there. But as a whole the land was not yet anywhere near stocked. No wonder men waited on the far side of the river, their hands sweaty with impatience as they bided their time for the day they could come here legally and lay claim.

And the time would come; Justin had little doubt of that. This was a white man's world, and what the white man wanted he always took. It had ever been so and would ever be so, he figured. He had never pondered the moral issues. He simply took those things for facts that were historically obvious. He felt no personal guilt in this obvious wrong because it was a thing not of his doing, a thing that would have happened the same way if he had never been born.

Once when old Elijah Tankard was a little way ahead, Justin said quietly, "If this is Indian Territory it sure ain't like I expected. It looks pretty much like the other side of the river except not as developed yet."

"You expected to see Indian villages and tepees and stuff like that?"

"Well, it *is* Indian Territory."

"Didn't you ever hear of the Five Civilized Tribes? They was brought here from back east. They're not like the wild Indians out on the plains; they live in houses like the rest of us. They got towns like everybody else. They've had their own schools since before I was born, their own newspapers, their own law. They're a hell of a lot more civilized than the general run of white folks that've moved in amongst them, you can bet your last breath on that."

They skirted the few small settlements and they rode out of their way to avoid meeting people on the trail. Elijah Tankard was supposed to be along as guide, but it seemed to Justin that Dark knew this part of the country as well as the old farmer did. It was unlikely Tankard strayed far from his farm except on rare occasions when he had to make the long trip to Fort Smith.

Justin noticed that by afternoon the old farmer, who

had seemed to doze in the saddle off and on through the morning, began to look around with interest and perhaps concern.

"Gettin' closer now to where he lives," Dark said quietly to Justin. "Further we go now the more chance somebody'll see us with him. Ain't always healthy here to be seen with lawmen."

Once they heard a wagon and rode quickly off to one side of the trail, dismounting and concealing themselves in a heavy motte. Directly the wagon came into view, driven by an Indian wearing a flat-brimmed black hat. The Indian saw the horsetracks leading out of the road and he glanced suspiciously toward the motte. Justin felt sure he couldn't see them behind the heavy foliage. The Indian would be nervous awhile. This country was as infested with outlaws as with snakes. He was probably thinking that men who would hide along a public road might well have mischief on their mind. Likely as soon as he could do so surreptitiously, he reached down and brought up a rifle or shotgun into his lap.

Pity to scare a man this way, Justin thought.

That was one of the things Judge Parker had said he was working toward: the day when people—white or Indian—could live here and travel this land and fear nothing more than a runaway horse or a bolt of lightning.

About dusk Elijah Tankard said, "My place is just ahead, around that bend in the road. I best ride in first and be sure there's nobody around but family."

Sam Dark dismounted to stretch his legs. Justin didn't feel secure enough to chance it. He sat on his horse, warily watching the farmer ride down a twisting wagon road past a cornfield and toward a long house which lay in a grove of trees that indicated a spring. He said, "There's a dozen places between here and that house where somebody could hide and put a bullet in you."

"In *me?*"

"It's you they got it in for."

"If they killed me, they couldn't leave you around to testify."

Justin frowned. "That thought has run through my mind."

"There's lots of places back up the road they could've got us if they'd wanted to. They've let us come this far. I reckon either the old man's tellin' the truth or else he's got somethin' awful interestin' waitin' for us down at the house."

"If that's the case, what do you plan to do?"

"Just go see what it is. When the other man holds all the cards only thing you can do is stand easy and stay awake."

Elijah Tankard returned up the road, shoulders slumped in weariness. He raised one hand as he neared the motte, a peace sign from his Indian in-laws. "Everything's fine down at the house. They're fixin' supper. Youall come on."

Sam Dark glanced at Justin and nodded. He swung into the saddle and pulled up even with the old man in the other rut of the wagon trail. Saddlegun across his lap, Justin hung back a length or two, following Dark so he could watch for any movement of the farmer's gun hand. He carefully watched on either side of the road, too, especially the cornfield where the rows came at oblique angles. A rabbit jumped up and skittered away into the green corn. By reflex Justin had the saddlegun halfway to his shoulder before he caught himself. If Dark or the old man sensed it neither gave any sign. Justin lowered the gun and rubbed a hand across his sweaty face. He wondered how Dark could be so icy calm.

The log house looked much like the one Justin had known at home. It had, from appearance, started with a single cabin, later augmented by a second section separated from the first by an open dog-run. Eventually, with passage of time and perhaps after the birth of the daughter, the dog-run was closed in for another room and the cabin stood now as a solid unit. Its sections did not match, but that was probably of no real concern to anybody. Its purpose was utility, not decoration.

A floorless overhang served as substitute for a porch. Beneath its roof stood a young man, his shoulders stiff and square, his eyes openly hostile. It had been too dark that night in Fort Smith for Justin to have seen what color Matthew Tankard's eyes were, if it had mattered. It startled him to see that despite the strongly Indian features and darker hue of his face the grim eyes were a deep blue. The color seemed out of place, a legacy from his white father.

Sam Dark studied the young farmer. "I didn't come here for trouble with you. But if that's what you got in mind, let's get done with it."

Matthew Tankard's jaw clenched. He glanced at his father and he said nothing.

Sam Dark swung down, stretching his tired legs again. Justin waited till he was sure Dark was on balance, then he dismounted too. He kept his gaze on Matthew Tankard, for he felt that he was where the threat lay, if there was one.

"Fellers," said the old man, "the womenfolks'll have supper ready directly. You-all want to unsaddle your horses and feed them a dab?"

Justin glanced at Dark. "What about them whiskey peddlers?"

The farmer put in, "Matthew went and took a look at them this afternoon. They're still right where they was, sellin' to all who come. They'll keep."

Justin was hungry, sure enough, but he doubted he would enjoy supper much. He looked to Sam Dark to see what the older deputy would do.

"Much obliged," Dark said. "The horses need rest and a bit of feed. So do we all. Way I figure it them peddlers can wait till tomorrow."

Justin blinked. "Tomorrow?"

"If we was to take them now we'd have them on our hands all night. We're too wore out. First time we let up our guard they'd be gone. So we'll stay here and rest if Mister Tankard and his womenfolks don't object. Come mornin' we'll be up ahead of the rooster."

Whoever said an Indian didn't show expression hadn't seen many Indians, Justin thought. The expression in Matthew Tankard's face left no doubt what he thought about the deputies spending the night. He turned to protest but his father ignored him. "Dark, that's just what I was fixin' to suggest."

"We can sleep someplace away from the house," Dark said. "Any company that comes in the night, they won't stumble over us."

They led the horses toward the log barn and the brush pens. Justin had a hard time holding his tongue until they were out of earshot. "I can feel that Indian boy's knifeblade on my Adam's apple."

Dark didn't ruffle. "All life is a gamble. Day you was born your mother gambled her life for yours. Your folks gambled whether they'd be able to feed you till you was old enough to make your own way. You gamble every day you live till finally one day you make that last bet and it don't pay. Everybody loses sooner or later."

"What if it comes *your* time and I happen to be standin' there?"

"That's what gives life its flavor, boy."

A washstand stood by the door. The Tankard girl walked up from the spring, toting water in an oaken bucket. She set the bucket on the washstand, her eyes sharply telling the deputies they'd damn well better use it before they went into the house.

"Much obliged," Dark said. Her eyes held the same ungiving hostility Justin had seen in her brother's. She wore a washed-out cotton dress like any farm girl, but it didn't hide the fact that she was half Indian. Her skin had a brownish hue and her facial structure showed the Cherokee ancestry. Her hair was braided Indian style, the braids reaching almost to her waist. And though she wore the dress as a concession to the father's blood, her feet were in beaded moccasins.

It was her eyes that startled Justin. Like her brother's they were blue.

Dress her up in a white woman's way from head to foot, comb out her hair, and you could almost pass her off as a sunburned white girl, Justin thought. In his mind he was doing her a compliment. It didn't occur to him that she probably would have no desire to do so, that she had

not the slightest regret for the part of her that was
Indian.

"Supper's waitin'," she said. "When you've cleaned
up."

Justin had half expected to hear only a grunt from her,
judging by her Indian look. But her speech was that of
her father—without accent, without effort. He thought
resentfully, *I expect we'll be clean enough for an Indian
place*, but he didn't put it into words. He had a notion it
wouldn't take much to provoke her into a fight. She
might be figuring on it anyway, but he saw no use
pushing her into it.

He kept watch until Dark had finished washing and
had wiped his face and hands dry on a big raw-edged
cloth hanging at the washstand. The cloth had been used
before. The girl had fetched clean water but she was
pleased to have them dry on an old towel. Dark caught
Justin's angry look.

"Put yourself in their place and figure we're lucky,
button. In their minds they got reason enough to kill
us—*me*, anyway. But they ain't done it and I don't think
they got any such notion."

"Right now they want to use us."

"Don't forget we're usin' them too. Think I'd of come
if I hadn't wanted so bad to get my hands on them
peddlers? I wouldn't of set foot on this place for all the
gold coin in the Territory after what I already done to
these folks."

Elijah Tankard appeared in the doorway. "You-all
come on in." His manner was more of tolerance than of
welcome.

Justin followed Dark, still wary. He glanced distrustfully at Matthew Tankard, trying to determine whether
the young man carried a weapon. If he did it wasn't
apparent. Dark made a slight bow toward the aging
Indian woman. His voice apologetic. "Miz Tankard, we
appreciate you fixin' for us. You didn't have to."

She tried, but she couldn't bring herself to look at him
without wavering. "You catch those peddlers. You do the
same to them that you did to my boy Barney."

Dark looked down uncomfortably. "Ma'am, we'll do the best we can."

Justin was a little surprised, hearing Dark address an Indian woman as "ma'am." Most people looked down on Indians, sort of the way they did on George Grider. They didn't "sir" a man or "ma'am" a woman. But then Sam Dark wasn't like just everybody else.

Justin had been a little concerned over the kind of meal to expect in a largely Indian household. From stories he had heard he wouldn't have been surprised to be presented dog stew. He found he needn't have worried. The Tankard women had fixed cornbread, beans, pork, thick black coffee. Justin ate slowly at first, watching the family, still not convinced they didn't have treachery on their minds. He had a wild thought that they might have poisoned the food, but he shed that notion when he saw the Tankards eating, especially old Elijah. The ride had famished him. Justin gave in to his own hunger and eased his watchfulness enough to put away a big supper.

The girl Naomi sat across the table. Every so often Justin sneaked a glance at her. Once he found her looking at him and quickly jerked his gaze away. He had seen a few Indians in his life, for they crossed the Arkansas settlements now and again, but he had never seen an Indian girl he thought to be pretty. He couldn't make up his mind about this one, not entirely. He decided if she weren't Indian he would consider her to be at least attractive. She would look better if she would get rid of the resentment in her eyes.

Hate me, then, if it makes you feel better. We'll be out of here tomorrow and you can go back to your paint and feathers.

After supper the old man offered them tobacco. It appeared to be homegrown. Dark accepted, though Justin knew the deputy had tobacco with him that had been bought in town and probably would be a tastier blend. Dark and the farmer sat and puffed, glancing at each other now and again, each wanting to talk but denied by the barrier that stood between them. Justin had looked up several times during supper at a tintype on the mantel over the fireplace. Afterwards he tried to slip across inconspicuously for a closer look. The picture was of an Indian in white man's full dress suit. Justin pondered the incongruity of it.

The girl said, "My mother's father. My grandfather."

"How did they get him dressed up thataway?"

He could tell immediately that he had insulted her. She said crisply, "He always went like that. He taught school."

Justin tolerated the close atmosphere as long as he could then went outside. Directly he heard the door open and he turned quickly. Matthew Tankard and his sister stood staring at him. In the dark, where the color of the eyes didn't show, Matthew looked pure Indian. The look was ominous to Justin.

"Stand easy, lawman," Matthew said in a voice like his father's, except younger. "We don't intend to fight you."

Justin looked from one to the other and weighed his words before he spoke. "Comin' to this place wasn't no idea of mine."

"Mine either, or Naomi's. If it was up to me we'd just slip out there and cut those peddlers' throats like my ancestors would've done. We'd bury them someplace nobody'd find them and then we'd be the dumbest bunch of Indians you ever saw. But Papa says that ain't the way; we got to call in the same law that killed our brother."

"Sam Dark is just doin' his job. And I'm tryin' to do mine."

"And so is Judge Parker. And so is his hangman. And so are them peddlers out yonder sellin' slow death to our people. Pretty world, ain't it?"

"It's all the world we got. Maybe we can make a better one out of it."

The girl said, "It *was* a better world, once, for the Indian. Till the white man came and spoiled it."

"You're half white."

The girl glanced at her brother. "We don't brag about it."

"Your daddy is all white. Where does that leave him?"

"He married into the Cherokees. He has more of their ways than of the white man."

"I'm white. Where does that leave me?" A little of exasperation was in his voice now.

The girl shook her head. "I don't know. Where do you *want* it to leave you?"

Dark came out eventually. He said nothing, just started for the barn. Justin followed. Dark scattered a little hay on the ground and unrolled his blanket. Justin did likewise, asking no questions until Dark wrapped a blanket around himself and rolled over, closing eyes. Then Justin said, "Did you see the way them people was lookin' at us? They hate us."

Dark didn't answer. Justin went on, "That girl's eyes . . . she could carve us up like catfish on a riverbank."

"You expect me to stay awake all night and keep watch?"

"I thought we might take turn about."

"When these people decide to fight us again they'll do it in broad daylight and facin' us. Better get yourself some rest."

In a few minutes Dark was asleep. It took Justin a lot longer.

V

At something like four in the morning Dark shook Justin's shoulder. "Roll out." Justin got up slowly, rubbing his eyes. Sleep held on like a drug, for he had lain awake much of the night worrying about the Tankards. He stopped at the washstand in front of the house. Splashing cold water over his face helped bring him awake. The fact that he was still alive, that nobody had come to bother them in the night, made him feel a little foolish. He wished he had slept when he had the chance.

They ate a breakfast of pork and fried bread and dark gravy, then saddled their horses. The farmer and his son went along.

Dark cautioned the bent-shouldered Elijah Tankard, "Now, you-all stay out of it. You got to go on livin' here and there's no use puttin' you in danger of trouble after we're gone. Any fightin' to be done it's our job, not yours. That's what they pay us such a big wage for."

The farmer frowned. "Me and Matthew, we was talkin' last night. We agreed you'd have a right smart better case if you was to catch them fellers actually a-sellin' whiskey. We thought me and Matthew would go in and buy some."

"You ever bought any whiskey off of them before?"

"Marshal, you know I don't hold with that. Been my aim all along to keep them peddlers out of our country."

"So if they know you they'd be suspicious, you all of a sudden comin' to buy. But your boy here, they'd maybe

46

expect it on account of him bein' Indian." He looked
apologetically at Matthew. "No offense meant."

Matthew ground his teeth together. "None taken. We
both know how the white man thinks."

"It'd look natural if you was to go in there smellin' of
the stuff and actin' like you'd been on an all-night drunk
and run out of drinkin'-whiskey. They'd be so anxious to
find out how much money they could fleece you out of
they wouldn't notice us till too late."

"How am I goin' to smell of whiskey? I ain't got none."

"I got some," Dark said. "Always carry a drop or two.
Never know when a man might come upon a snake."

Justin frowned. "I thought it was against the law for
anybody to carry whiskey into the Territory."

"It is."

"You're carryin' it."

"That law is for *people.*"

They rode half an hour. Matthew Tankard raised his
hand. "Down yonder in that thicket, that's where they're
camped at."

It was still so dark that Justin could hardly make out
the heavier gray of the dense foliage. He caught a faint
smell of smoke from what was left of last night's campfire,
the coals banked against the morning's need.

Sam Dark studied the layout, as much as he could see
of it. "Mister Tankard, I'd rather you stayed up here,
plumb out of it. They don't need to know about you. Me
and Justin, we'll slip down into that thicket and get
ourselves set while it's still dark. Matthew, you wait till
good daylight, then start singin' and ride in. Act drunk.
Minute you pay them and they hand you the goods we'll
move. You step back and out of the way. Far as they need
to know you had nothin' to do with us."

"Where's that whiskey I'm supposed to smell like?"

Dark brought a small bottle out of his saddlebag.
"Before you go in pour a little on your clothes. Swish a
little around in your mouth. I don't have to tell you not
to swallow it."

Matthew's voice was testy. "You didn't have to, but you
did tell me anyhow."

"No offense meant."

Matthew looked down, irritated. "None taken."

Dark tied his horse and leisurely circled to enter the thicket well above the camp. Justin followed close behind him, excitement beginning to play up and down his back. At length Dark paused, crouching behind heavy brush. Justin dropped down upon his belly and peered through the gradually lifting darkness. He could see a wagon and a staked team and two bedrolls, the men sleeping with their feet toward the embers of last night's campfire. Dark leaned to whisper in Justin's ear. "You stay here. I'll slip on around to the far side of the wagon. When you see me get up and start in you come too. And be ready; you never know what a man'll do."

·Dark left him and faded out of sight. Justin lay waiting, hand sweaty-cold on his pistol. Daylight came slower than he had ever seen it in his life, the darkness taking what seemed like hours to lift. Rosy streaks finally reached across the eastern sky. The sun came up, bathing the camp in eye-pinching light. One of the men stirred in his bedroll, turning a couple of times and then flinging his blankets aside. He sat up scratching his chest, then scratching his tangled hair and his scraggy growth of beard. He took a long drink from a nearby jug, rolled himself a cigarette and drew a long drag or two from it. he took his boots out from under the blanket where they had been placed to protect them from the dew. Justin heard him call to his partner to rouse his lazy something-or-other and go punch up the fire.

Justin looked up toward the hill, wondering when Matthew would ride down out of the sunrise. It was a while before he heard from far off a strange song that he took to be some kind of Indian chant. The men in camp looked at each other. One walked over to the wagon to fetch a rifle. Silhouetted in red against the early morning sun Matthew Tankard sat his horse a moment, then started down. He sang a discordant chant and slumped loosely in his saddle. The sun picked up a momentary glint from the bottle in his hand. Sam Dark's bottle. The two peddlers watched him curiously.

Riding into the edge of camp Matthew turned the bottle upside down to show that it was empty. He held it to his mouth and tilted it as if to lick away any last drop that might previously have escaped him. Then he flung the bottle aside and shouted, "You got whiskey?"

The men eyed him suspiciously. The one with the rifle held it pointed at Matthew. "What you want, Injun?"

"Friend give me bottle. Tell me he buy bottle from you. Now I want to buy bottle from you. You got whiskey?"

"Kind of early in the mornin', ain't it?" one demanded.

The other walked close to Matthew for a good look. "Not for this one it ain't. It's still late at night. Smells like a still." To Matthew he said, "Maybe we got whiskey. You got money?"

Matthew slid down awkwardly from the saddle, going to one knee and grabbing at his stirrup to catch himself. "Sure, I got money. You think I'm some damn broke Indian?" He dug around in his pockets and came up with a couple of silver dollars. The peddler shook his head. "Not enough, Injun. Takes a heap sight more than that for our whiskey. This is good stuff, not some cheap farmyard squeezin. You got three more of them dollars we might do business."

Five dollars. Little as Justin knew about whiskey he knew this was robbery. No wonder these peddlers liked to work the Territory.

Matthew dug some more. He dropped one coin to the ground. Both men stepped forward eagerly to pick it up.

He's sure got their whole attention now, Justin thought. *We could walk the whole United States Army in here and they wouldn't see it.*

Matthew came up with the five dollars. One of the peddlers reached for it but Matthew pulled his hands back. "First you give-um whiskey."

The taller of the two jerked his head toward the wagon. "Go fetch it, Willis."

The one named Willis brought a bottle. Matthew took it and held out his hand as if to pay. Then he drew it back. "One bottle not enough. How much more dollars for two bottles."

"Five dollars."

"No got five more. For two bottle, maybe you sell-um cheaper."

The peddlers were engrossed now in haggling with Matthew. Justin glanced toward the place where he knew Sam Dark was waiting. Dark raised up cautiously, pausing to be sure he would not be observed too soon, then moved forward, saddlegun in his hands. Justin pushed to his feet, wiped his sweaty hands on his shirt and took a good grip on his pistol as he stepped out to meet Dark. The peddlers were still arguing with Matthew. Sam Dark was within two paces of them before he spoke.

"Raise your hands. You're under arrest."

The two whirled. One grabbed at his waist, but his pistol belt still lay on his bedroll. He hadn't gotten around to putting it on. The other stood stiff, hands half upraised, eyes startled. He had laid down his rifle. It was too far to reach. The surprise faded, and anger took its place. "Who the hell are you?"

"Federal marshals," Dark replied. "You're under arrest for sellin' whiskey to an Indian."

Matthew Tankard backed away, still holding the bottle and the silver dollars.

Sam Dark ordered the two men to lie on their bellies, their hands over their heads. One promptly complied. The other stood defiant until Dark moved menacingly toward him. The man sank to his knees, cursing, then finally to his stomach. Dark handed his saddlegun to Justin and leaned over the men, quickly searching them for weapons. He found nothing except a long knife, which he took. "Justin, you chase back up the hill and fetch our horses down. We'll need the handcuffs."

Justin did as he was told, the excitement running through him like floodwater down a draw. He found Elijah Tankard sitting on the hill, watching. "Everything go the way you-all figured?" the farmer asked.

"Seems like." He caught the horses. "You best stay put so nobody ties you into this."

Justin rode down, leading Dark's horse. He tied the animals to the wheels of the wagon and brought out the handcuffs. The men lay with arms outstretched. Dark motioned for Justin to put the handcuffs on them. It was easy but he remained wary, half expecting one of the men to jump up and challenge him.

"All right," Dark said when the men were cuffed, "you two can get up now. It's a long ways to Fort Smith."

"We ain't even had coffee," whimpered the peddler named Willis. He didn't seem overly bright. Justin guessed he was probably the swamper of the pair, brought along to do the heavy lifting and the dirty work.

The other glowered at Matthew. "Damn stupid Indian."

Matthew Tankard dropped all pretense of drunkenness. Gone, too, was any pretense that he had not been in league with the lawmen. His mouth took on a sardonic smile. "Not so stupid. Maybe you'd like a drink of your own whiskey." He made no effort now at the broken English people expected to hear from an Indian. He stepped over to Willis and extended the bottle he had bought. "You can have it back. I'll keep my five dollars."

"Matthew," Dark warned, "don't . . ."

The other peddler was quick. He reached for the bottle but grabbed Matthew's hand instead. The bottle smashed on the ground as the man twisted Matthew's arm and brought the Indian around backward. In one quick motion the man snaked the pistol out of Matthew's belt and brought it to bear on Dark, using Matthew as a shield.

"All right, lawman, drop that gun or I'll kill this Injun too dead to skin!" Dark lowered the saddlegun, cursing under his breath.

Matthew was stunned, but only for a moment. He brought up his booted foot and stomped down on the peddler's toes.

Justin hadn't lowered the pistol. As the peddler was

momentarily distracted Justin rushed in, hoping to get past Matthew and jam the pistol into the man's ribs. Then he could fire if he had to, and he wouldn't hit Matthew by error. But the peddler saw him coming. He swung Matthew's pistol around and jerked the trigger. Justin saw the flash and felt something strike his head like a sledgehammer. He heard another shot and felt an impact to his shoulder. He spun around, seeing crazy flashing lights, and he tasted dirt as he fell on his face. He was vaguely aware of fast movement around him, and he thought he heard another shot. He was too far gone to know.

Sometime later he felt something cold on his face and became conscious of hands wiping his forehead with a wet cloth. He opened his eyes but saw only a painful, blinding light. He shut them quickly. His head felt as if someone had struck him with the sharp edge of an axe. And someone had built a blazing fire in his shoulder.

Sam Dark's voice was quiet and gentle. "Easy there, button. Just you lay there. Movin' is only goin' to hurt you."

It was a while before Justin could begin to orient himself. At first he had an odd notion he was back on the farm and a mule had kicked him. Gradually he began to realize he had left the family place weeks ago. Piece by piece he worked out the fact that he and Sam Dark had come here hunting for whiskey peddlers. He realized finally that one of them had shot him. Opening his eyes cautiously he found he could see a little. He could discern the worried face of Sam Dark, leaning over him. A couple more men stood nearby. He couldn't make out the faces, but he reasoned that they had to be the Tankards.

"Shot me, didn't he?" Justin asked weakly.

"Twice." Dark tried to smile, but it was thin. "Hit you once in the head. That wouldn't have caused much damage, but he put another bullet in your shoulder."

"Did he get away?"

"No."

Justin turned his head a little. Now he could see the

peddler—the man named Willis—handcuffed to a wagonwheel. Another lay in the clearing, crumpled like a rag doll carelessly flung aside.

Dark said, "I couldn't shoot because of Matthew. But Mister Tankard, he shot him from the top of the hill."

Unnerved, the old farmer said, "I shot a man once in the big war. Never done it again in my whole life until today."

Matthew Tankard knelt beside Justin. "I pulled a fool stunt, showin' off to that peddler, tryin' to show him us Indians can do somethin' besides drink poison. I like to've got you killed."

Justin's left arm wouldn't move. He reached up with his right hand and touched his throbbing head. The wound was warm and sticky to his touch. His hand came away bloody.

Dark said, "Lay back, button. We got to stop you from bleedin' before we can move you any."

Justin became aware he was lying on a blanket. The sky rocked back and forth, strangely red instead of blue. He shut his eyes, hoping things would stabilize, that the burning pain might diminish. "I don't understand," he murmured. "A little time in jail . . . I don't see why he'd of took the chance."

Dark said, "Peddlin' whiskey ain't the worst some of these people have done. Likely he was wanted for somethin' a lot more serious. Probably why he was out in the Territory in the first place. Knew if we got him to Fort Smith he'd be tried for somethin' else besides whiskey runnin' and that Judge Parker would stand him on that gallows with a rope around his neck."

"A bullet was too good for him," Matthew Tankard gritted.

Dark replied, "Too bad we got this other one here to witness. Otherwise I could report that I shot him."

Matthew frowned. "You want the credit, Dark?"

"It's no credit. But if I'd shot him instead of your daddy doin' it, it might've saved you-all some worry later on." He glanced at the old farmer. "You-all will be marked now amongst the peddlers."

The farmer said soberly, "It ain't a good feelin' to kill a
man, even if he *did* deserve it. But I was in this country
before his kind of trash ever come. I'll be here when
they're gone."

Justin clenched his teeth as Sam Dark bathed the two
wounds in whiskey out of the wagon. Justin wondered if
the stuff might be poison. It didn't matter to the
peddlers, once they got their money, if some of their
customers went blind or died. The whiskey burned like
the hinges of hell and Justin lapsed almost into unconsciousness. He was dimly aware that Sam was probing
the shoulder wound, and later that he was wrapping it
with cloth from the wagon. Justin knew the cloth was
probably more dangerous than the whiskey but he was in
no condition to protest. He could hear Dark and the
Tankards agreeing that the thing to do now was to take
Justin to the Tankard farm in the peddlers' wagon. To
make room for him they pitched the whiskey bottles and
jugs out. Elijah Tankard picked up an axe and solemnly
smashed those that didn't break in the fall. Dark
salvaged a few to keep for medicinal purposes.

The prisoner Willis had regained courage now, satisfied they wouldn't murder him out of hand. "Listen to
me, farmer! They'll make you pay for every drop of that
stuff!"

Tankard gripped the axe as if considering swinging it at
the man. "We've already paid. More than you'll ever
know."

Matthew Tankard pointed at the dead man. "What'll
we do about him?"

"Throw a blanket over him," Dark said. "Damn if I'll
put him in the wagon with that button. We can come
back later and bury him here."

During this time Justin lay still, the sky swaying
dizzily back and forth whenever he opened his eyes. He
didn't open them much.

He heard Matthew Tankard call, "Somebody's comin'
yonder, Dark. Couple of wagons on the trail."

Justin tried to raise up and look. He couldn't move
anything but his head. He turned it, trying vainly to see.

Dark touched him gently. "Lay still. Just lay still." Soon Justin could hear the creak of wagons and the rattle of chains and the plodding of horses. He could tell that Dark was staying behind the peddler wagon, out of sight, letting the other wagons get close before he showed himself.

"The devil's own luck," Dark said, half under his breath. "Them is Harvey Oates' wagons. Harvey Oates, the worst whiskey runner in Indian Territory."

Elijah Tankard and Matthew stood in the open but within easy talking distance of Dark. Matthew said, "All we done so far has been to cut off the tail of the snake. Now we got a chance to chop off its head."

"No," Dark told him.

Matthew said, "I see one man on each wagon, three men on horses. That's five. No, yonder's another man bringin' up the rear. That's six. It's two to one, them against us."

Dark replied firmly, "It's *nothin'* to one; you ain't goin' to contest them. Matthew, I want you and your daddy to stay out of the way. You're no match for the kind of men Oates keeps around him."

"You can't fight them by yourself."

"I know. If it looks like a fight I'll back off. I never play in a game where the other man has stacked the cards. See that ugly one on the dun horse? That's Quarternight. He's a gun fighter and a bad one. And that Negro? That's Huff. They say he's got whip marks all over his back from the slave days, when he was still little. It made him mean. Harvey keeps him and Quarternight for protection."

The prisoner Willis decided the men at the wagons were near enough to hear him. He shouted, "Harvey, look out! It's a marshal!"

The wagon drivers hauled up. The men on horseback moved together, conferred, and then one rode forward, trailed by the others. The man in the lead held a rifle across his saddle and his eyes were watchful. Justin could see him now, through a crimson haze. Harvey

Oates surely must be able to see that Willis was handcuffed to the wagon wheel, Justin thought.

"What goes on here?" Oates demanded.

Sam Dark stepped out into sight, saddlegun in his hands. "Howdy, Harvey. Didn't figure on runnin' into you so far out here in the Territory."

"I asked you what's goin' on here?"

"Friends of yours had a little trouble. I caught them sellin' firewater."

Harvey Oates was a big man with a red face, broad nose and hair in his ears. Heavy black eyebrows framed a pair of belligerent eyes. "Sam, I don't know that man."

"He called you Harvey. Sounded familiar."

"I been workin' this country a long time, haulin' freight. Lots of people know me, people I don't know atall. You talked like there was more of them. I don't see but one."

"Other one's lyin' yonder under a blanket. He's dead."

Anger leaped into Oates' eyes. But he kept a calm voice. "It don't mean nothin' to me. I got no friends in this camp."

"I don't believe that, Harvey. I figure they are customers of yours, or maybe even on your payroll. I figure you got more whiskey in them wagons. I figure you're out restockin' the peddlers."

The ugly one, Quarternight, glanced at Oates and pulled his horse up closer in silent challenge. Close beside him sat the third rider, the large Negro, whose right hand rested on his gun butt. Outlaws of every race found their way into the Territory. Oates glared at Sam Dark. "Figure all you want to. The point is, you don't know. Figurin' don't carry no weight in court."

"I thought maybe I'd take a look, Harvey."

Oates leaned back in the saddle and glanced toward the two horsemen flanking him. "I bet you ain't got no warrant to be lookin' in my wagons."

"I could get one."

"But you ain't *got* one. If you want to inspect my wagons you better head for Fort Smith and get you a warrant. Then you can look all you want to."

"Meanwhile you'd get shed of all your whiskey."

"You're figurin' again, Sam. Figurin' ain't provin', is it?" A harsh smile came to Oates' face, for he could tell he had all the advantage. "Sam, I've always went out of my way to be friendly with you. I never did know just what you held against me."

"You *do* know. It's out there in your wagons."

"You ain't seen nothin'. Get yourself a warrant and then we'll let you look. Now we're fixin' to move on down this road. You figurin' on standin' in our way?"

Sam Dark tried to stare the big man down. It came out a draw. "I'll stop you, Harvey. Not today, but one of these times."

Oates spat. "Well if it ain't goin' to be today I'd be much obliged if you'd move yourself out of our road."

Dark moved back reluctantly. Oates turned in his saddle and motioned for the wagons to come ahead. He and Quarternight sat on their horses and stared at Sam Dark as the wagons went by. When they were past Oates pulled on the reins and made his horse back up a step. "I'll see you in Fort Smith sometime, Sam, and I'll buy you a drink. A legal drink."

The prisoner at the wheel saw that Oates was not going to help him. "Harvey," he called anxiously, "you just goin' to leave me thisaway?"

Oates stopped. "Stranger, there ain't nothin' I can do for you. But I'll give you some advice. Sit tight and don't tell nobody nothin'. I bet you got friends in Fort Smith, and I bet by the time Sam gets you to town they'll have a good lawyer hired and waitin' for you."

Willis nodded, relieved. "Harvey, it was that old farmer yonder that shot Mitch. And that Indian boy with him, he helped these lawmen set the whole thing up."

Oates frowned at the Tankards. "Seems to me I know you, don't I? Name's Tankard, ain't it, farmer?" His eyes narrowed in malice. "None of my business, but I'm glad I ain't in your shoes. Some people around here don't take kindly to them that helps people like Sam Dark. Some have got a long memory."

Elijah said bitterly, "I had a boy named Barney. Is your memory that long, Oates?"

Oates shook his head. "Like I said, it's none of my business."

He rode after his wagons, the two gunmen flanking him. They talked as they rode, and Quarternight looked back once toward the Tankards.

Elijah said finally, "Too bad there was so many of them. I bet you was right about them wagons, Dark."

Dark nodded. He and Matthew Tankard carefully lifted Justin into the wagon and made him as comfortable as was possible on a pair of blankets. Dark started to put the prisoner Willis in with Justin but thought better of it. "The hell with him," he said. "A walk'll do him a world of good." He uncuffed the man from the wagon wheel and locked him to the rod that fastened the endgate of the wagon. "He'll be too busy keepin' up to study on any mischief."

Willis cursed. "You aimin' to make me walk plumb to Fort Smith? That's an awful long ways."

"Longer than you ever realized," Dark agreed. "But we won't go all the way today. That button needs to lay up and rest. As for you and me we'll wait at the Tankards' till George Grider shows up with the tumbleweed wagon." He glanced at the farmer. "That is, if it's all right with you."

Elijah nodded his gray head. "You and this boy here, you've earned anything you want to ask for."

They went to the Tankards' place, Dark driving the wagon, the prisoner walking along behind, complaining, threatening, begging. The Tankards followed, leading the extra horses. The jolting brought jarring pain to Justin Moffitt, but there was nothing he or Dark could do about it. Justin fought back tears. He had not felt such despair since the first night he had left the family farm and had camped alone by the bank of some unknown creek to eat a dismal supper and lie sleepless, listening to the wild cries of the night-roaming creatures. Justin was aware that his wound was bleeding some and he knew he could very well die. Fever was rising and in his misery the despair deepened. He opened his eyes and looked out the back of the wagon, past the protesting prisoner to Matthew Tankard, who appeared once again all Indian as he brought up the rear. He closed his eyes and saw visions of the farm and wished he were there. It had never looked so good to him in reality as it did now in the homesick glow of memory.

Sometime later he awoke, startled to find that he had either slept or lapsed into unconsciousness. The wagon was not moving. He heard Sam Dark unlocking the prisoner from the tailgate and moving him around to the side of the wagon, snapping the cuff shut over a spoke in the wheel. Willis cried anxiously, "What if that team takes a notion to run away with me shackled here?"

"Then," Dark said coldly, "you better be a hell of a runner."

Justin gritted his teeth against the pain as they lifted him over the tailgate and carried him into the house. Fevered, he could nevertheless see the two women hurrying out the door. Elijah said, "Dawn . . . Naomi . . . you women got a job to do."

They placed Justin on a wooden-frame bed and a cornshuck mattress. "My brother's bed," said Matthew. "Hope it's good enough for you."

Justin couldn't tell whether there was sarcasm in the young Indian's voice or not. At the moment he was too sick to care. He felt Naomi Tankard's deft fingers removing the cloth Sam Dark had wrapped around his shoulder, and she was cleansing the wound again. It didn't seem so painful now as when Dark had done it. The fever had dulled him.

Elijah Tankard matter-of-factly told the women what had happened. Justin could feel Naomi's hands go stiff. "Papa, you killed a man?" When he reiterated that he had she said, "And those other people, they know you did it?" He told her they did. She spoke gravely, "Papa . . ."

The older woman began talking, or perhaps it was some kind of chant. Justin couldn't tell because the words were strange. Cherokee, he reasoned.

Sam Dark had watched in silence while the women took away the bloody cloths he had put on Justin. "No bullet in there," he said. "I looked. It went clean through."

When the women had rebound Justin's wounds, Sam Dark stood up. "Mister Tankard . . . Matthew . . . I'm goin' to ask another favor. It'll be days before we can move that button without risk to his life."

"He's welcome here," said Elijah.

"I figured he would be. Now, I'd like to leave our prisoner here with you awhile, too."

"You goin' someplace, Dark?"

"Thought I'd trail after them wagons awhile."

Matthew asked, "What you got in mind?"

"Nothin' definite. Just thought I'd go and watch. I might get lucky."

"I'll go with you."

"No, that'd leave your daddy too much responsibility all by himself." He paused, looking at Justin. "Besides, whatever I do I've at least got a badge to justify me. You'd be on your own."

Justin tried to raise his hand, tried to protest against Dark going off and leaving him here among strangers. But he couldn't get the words said. He could hear Dark walking out, explaining that George Grider should be along by tomorrow sometime, bringing the tumbleweed wagon, and that Dark expected to be back by then.

Sometime after that Justin lapsed into sleep. When at last he awakened, he saw a candle flickering on a small table near the bed. He sensed a presence and turned his head slowly. Naomi Tankard sat rocking in a chair. Seeing he was awake she stopped rocking. Justin tried to raise himself up but couldn't. He lay blinking, trying again to orient himself. "Be still," she said. "Any movin' you try to do just makes it worse."

His head was hammering. He reached up cautiously with his right hand and felt a bandage wrapped around his forehead. "I can't help feelin' like that feller *did* shoot out some of my brains after all. I oughtn't be just layin' here."

"I don't see that you got any choice."

"Is Mister Dark back yet?"

"No."

"Sure wish he was. Wisht he'd stayed here to begin with."

"You don't think he'll come back for you?"

"He'll be here unless somethin' happens to him. I just wisht he was here. I think we've brought trouble for you folks."

"There's been trouble here before."

"Folks say these Territory outlaws, they stick together."

"So do us Indians."

Justin lay quiet, trying to think. "Funny, I'd sort of forgot you was Indian atall."

"Had you?" she sounded dubious.

"You talk . . . well, you talk just like everybody else."

"Not like everybody. I can talk two languages, English and Cherokee. Can you?"

"No," Justin admitted ruefully. "I reckon I talk English as good as nearly anybody, but I sure don't speak no Cherokee."

"So bein' white don't make you better than anybody else, does it?"

"I never said . . ."

"Yes, you did. With your eyes, the way you looked at us when you came here yesterday. You said it."

"I'm sorry. I didn't go to cause you grief."

"It didn't upset me any. I only worry about the opinions of people I like."

He burned under the scorn in her voice. "I didn't ask to come here, you know. I come on orders, And I wouldn't of got shot at all if your brother . . ." He stopped himself, for he saw the futility of argument. Her mind was made up and talking wouldn't change it. He hurt badly enough without compounding the misery by flaring up this way. He turned his head away a minute, then back again to look at her, somehow wanting to make her feel kindlier toward him. "Look, if it's any consolation to you I've never shot at an Indian in my life. The only ones I ever seen was just travelin' across the country, and when they'd ask us for somethin' to eat we always give it to them. My pa wasn't an Indian fighter, nor my grandpa nor any other of my kinfolks that I know anything about. We always let people alone and hoped they done the same for us."

She sat rocking, staring at him. He had heard the old fable that Indians never smiled, but she made a liar of it.

"You must be goin' to live," she said, "or you couldn't have gotten that mad."

Sometime after daylight Sam Dark rode in wearily, shoulders sagging. But even through the window Justin could see him grin. Elijah Tankard went out to meet him. Matthew Tankard walked down from the barn and reached for Dark's reins, wordlessly offering to take care of his horse. Justin heard Dark ask, "How's the button doin'?"

"A right smart better this mornin' but still feverin' some," the farmer replied. "How was your ride?"

"Tell you about it directly. Got any coffee?"

"Got coffee on and the women'll hustle up some breakfast. I'd judge by looks that you need it."

First thing Dark did was to come in and look at Justin. "Button, you think you're goin' to make it?"

"I expect so."

"I wasn't sure of it yesterday. Guess you got a harder head than we thought."

"You trailed them wagons. Find any whiskey in them?"

"Never did get to look. I'm satisfied the whiskey was hidden in the beds of the wagons and covered up with a lot of freight and trade goods."

"So you just had to let them go?"

"Didn't have no evidence I could take into court."

The old farmer took the news in dejection. "So Harvey Oates keeps on peddlin' ruination and linin' his pockets with silver."

"Not this trip." Dark sipped at a cup of hot coffee and a

thin smile came. "Seems like Harvey had an accident. Somehow or other a fire started durin' the night. Burned both of them wagons clean to the hubs."

Matthew Tankard had come into the room in time to hear most of it. "Lightnin', maybe."

Dark grinned. "Maybe."

VI

Later they heard horses and Dark went to the window expecting to see George Grider. Justin could hear him mutter. "It's Harvey Oates. Got his whole bunch with him." Through the open door Justin could see Oates and the gunman Quarternight. He took Dark's word that the others were there. He could see one teamster riding a workhorse bareback.

Dark told Justin, "You lay still, button. I doubt old Harvey'll make any trouble right now." He walked outside, motioning for the Tankards to stay in the house. The women did, but Elijah and Matthew moved out under the overhang. Justin raised up and dropped his legs off the side of the bed, then moved down far enough to watch out the open door. The voices came clear.

"Howdy, Harvey," Dark said when Oates came.

The prisoner was still handcuffed to the wheel of the whiskey wagon. He stood up, expecting release. But Oates gave him hardly a glance. His hard gaze rested on Dark. "You look kind of sleepy-eyed, Sam."

"Age," Dark replied. "I don't sleep good of a night anymore."

"Guilty conscience, maybe."

"Possible. I done things in my life that I wasn't proud of."

"Do anything last night that you ought to've thought over?"

"Can't think what it might've been."

Oates stared, his eyes hating Dark. "Sam, you're a long ways from Fort Smith."

"Not so far that the judge's rope won't reach."

"Somebody done us a bad turn last night. Somebody touched off both of our freight wagons. Now the judge is keen on doin' things legal."

"So am I, Harvey. If you want me to I'll go investigate."

"You needn't bother. It's done. But nobody'll catch me unawares again. Next time somebody'll catch a bellyful of buckshot that he'll be slow to digest. I doubt as the judge'll object to a man protectin' his property." He paused, his gaze moving to the Tankard men. "I reckon you folks was here all last night?"

Dark said, "I'll vouch for them."

Oates gritted, "I figured you would." He frowned at the old farmer. "Good ways to your next neighbor, ain't it?"

"It's not so far."

"I hear there's people in this country that don't like a man gettin' thick with the Fort Smith courthouse crowd. I hear it's considered a hazard to a man's health." He jerked his thumb toward the prisoner. "I expect even a whiskey peddler has got friends. They might not take kindly to what you done."

Elijah said, "We got no reason to care what they think."

"Looks to me like you got lots of reason. Old Sam Dark, he can't stay here all the time. But you got to."

Matthew Tankard took an angry step forward. "You threatenin' us?"

"No, Indian, not threatenin'. It don't mean a thing to me one way or the other. Just pointin' out facts."

Matthew took another step and Quarternight brought up a rifle lying across the pommel of his saddle. The big Negro edged his horse closer. Sam Dark reached forward and touched Matthew's shoulder. "Stand easy. They ain't got an ace in their hand. Don't give them one." He looked at Oates. "Water your horses, Harvey, then get movin'. These folks don't welcome you here."

"They may come to wish they'd welcome me instead of you."

In a minute they were gone, Quarternight looking grimly back over his shoulder. The prisoner at the wagon had a happier expression. "Farmer, you heard what he said. I got friends. If you was to turn me loose maybe they'd forget what you done to my partner."

Matthew seethed. "Let's *do* turn him loose, Indian style. Let's give him a three-minute start then see how far he can get before I catch up and kill him."

That sobered the prisoner who looked worriedly at Sam Dark. Dark said, "No, we got to keep it legal, the judge's way. Besides this is just a little fish. The big one has got away."

"He ain't gone far. We could catch him."

"And do what? When I take him before the judge I want to do it with evidence that'll hang him."

George Grider came eventually, all alone on the seat of that big freight wagon. It seemed almost a waste, all that mulepower going all that distance to haul back a single prisoner. The lanky Negro eased wearily down from the wagon and stretched himself, pressing hands against his sides. "Sure been a long ways." He shook with Sam Dark then balefully eyed the handcuffed man. "Where you got the rest of them hid?"

Dark said, "This is the only one we have."

Grider smiled. "Him? We could've took him to Fort Smith on a water cart. Old age must be gettin' you, Mister Sam."

"Maybe so."

"Where's the boy at?"

Dark led the way into the house. Grider took off his floppy hat and nodded politely at the Tankard men, giving a little extra surprised scrutiny to Matthew Tankard's Indian features. There was a sort of easy tolerance between Indian and Negro here in the Territory, though before the war some of the wealthier Indians had been slaveowners. Grider's eyes widened at sight of Justin lying on the bed. He eased a little when he found there were no potentially mortal wounds. He brought himself to make a crooked grin. "Boy, old judge is liable to fire you, layin' off on the job thataway."

Justin tried to think of something appropriate to say but there wasn't a funny streak in him. Grider said, "Might've been better if you'd got killed. You'd of gone on the hero list. This way you're just a laid-up deputy that the guv'ment's got to feed. They do git impatient."

Justin could sense deep concern behind the black man's banter. "I'll try to do better next time."

Grider said, "We got lots of room in the wagon. We can lay out a bed for you and you can keep the prisoner company on the way home."

Dark disagreed. "We better not try till he's better able to ride."

Justin frowned. "You fixin' to leave me here, Mister Dark?"

"You're not afraid of the Tankards, are you?"

"You know better than that."

"Well, then, it's settled. Me and George'll take the prisoner in. Longer he stays here the more apt he is to bring trouble down on the Tankards. You stay till you can ride then you come on in. You can find Fort Smith by yourself, can't you?"

Justin said impatiently, "How green do you think I am?"

"Don't you start till you know you're strong enough to make it. You're bein' paid to work, not to be layin' off on a roadside someplace."

The women fixed George Grider something to eat then he started east in the tumbleweed wagon, Dark following on horseback. The last thing Justin saw of them was the prisoner sitting shackled in the wagonbed, bouncing as the iron-rimmed wheel dropped into a rut. Justin could hear the cry of protest but didn't see George turn his head. The Negro was probably grinning and looking for another rut.

For a couple or three days Justin didn't move much. The first day it was too painful. Naomi Tankard brought him just about everything he needed. The second day the pain was less severe, but by then he had become used to Naomi fetching things and found he liked it. There didn't seem to be much gain in upsetting a favorable arrangement. Not that he tried to make things look worse than they were. The wound had swollen, and for a couple of days it had a red and angry look before the swelling started down and the healing set in.

By then Justin was walking around, though he wasn't doing it very fast. He figured the bullet had trimmed him close for he was a while regaining his balance. He never made more than a couple or three steps before he had to grab something—a chair, a bedstead, a table. Once he reached out and there wasn't anything to grab except Naomi. He did, and his face went suddenly warm. Hers colored a little. Quickly as he got his balance Justin jerked his hand away.

"Sorry. I didn't go to do that."

"No harm done, I suppose." She sounded as if she weren't sure.

"Don't want you to think I meant anything by it."

"You're not the type to grab an Indian girl."

"Not *any* girl." The warmth in his face was slow to ebb. "You always make out like I got somethin' against you for bein' Indian. Maybe the trouble is that you hold it against me for bein' white."

"I guess you can't help it."

He figured a half Indian family like this was bound to live somehow differently from other people, but after several days he could see little to support that theory. Occasionally they lapsed into Cherokee language but mostly they talked English, and it sounded the same as his own. The women cooked white man's food, the same as any farm family raising and eating most of its own produce. He had kept expecting to eat dog stew or something of the kind, but it didn't turn out that way. They said grace over their meals, a habit Justin had lost since leaving home. An uncle, Naomi said, was a minister.

Everybody in the Tankard family worked hard for there seemed more to be done than time to do it. Even so, Justin noted that Matthew always managed to take off and hunt. Late every day a full-blooded Indian of Matthew's age would show up, rifle in hand. He was introduced to Justin as cousin Blue Wing who lived a couple of miles over the hill. Usually they got back about dark carrying fresh meat. Matthew's Indian strain was strong when it came to hunting.

Justin tried to join the women at hoeing the garden, but they kept the hoes out of his reach until he got dizzy and had to go sit down. They told him plants responded better to a woman's touch than to a man's, an Indian notion Justin suspected had been originated by some Cherokee male whose hand fitted better the bow than the hoe.

Feeling came back into Justin's left arm and he found he could get limited use of his fingers. When old Elijah brought some harness from the barn and spread it beneath the shaded overhang Justin was able to help him mend it. That much, at least, he could do to help repay for bed and board. And that night when Matthew came home without meat, the front sight missing off of his rifle, Justin took a silver coin and laboriously fashioned a new sight from it. Matthew stared at him in surprise and with a little new respect.

Elijah watched approvingly. "You'd of been a good gunsmith. You ought to've taken up fixin' guns instead of shootin' them. You wouldn't be laid up the way you been."

Justin ran his fingers down the long barrel. It was an old rifle, a hand-me-down from before the big war. But it had been cared for, and in the hands of a careful shooter it could probably trim whiskers and not bring blood.

Matthew saw Justin's appreciation for the old weapon. "Like the gun do you, deputy? My old granddaddy—not the school-teachin' one—took that off a man in a fight. A white man." He paused, a harsh humor in his eyes. "My granddaddy scalped him."

Justin managed a half-hearted smile. "I expect it was a rifle worth fightin' for in its day."

"Still worth fightin' for. It could still fetch down a
trophy for a scalphunter."

Justin held the rifle toward him. "You lookin' at my
scalp?"

"I reckon not. They've taken all the fun out of life
these days. But my old granddaddy, he'd of taken it."

Elijah rebuked his son. "Hush up, Matthew. It's not
fitten to make light of death thataway."

"It comes to all of us, Papa, whether we take it light or
take it hard."

As his strength continued to build Justin started going
to the stock pens with Matthew and watching him break
horses. Matthew had a skill and ease at this trade, so he
broke horses for other people for a fee. It looked easy the
way Matthew did it. Justin considered trying to help him
but knew he would be refused. He had no business
boarding one of those broncs anyway. His proficiencies
were in work he could do with his hands, like smithing
and carpentry. He could ride a horse as well as most any
farm boy, but he was no bronc breaker and knew it. So
he contented himself with helping saddle a wild one or
with opening the gate so Matthew could ride a humped-
up pony out into the open pasture and give it its head.

Matthew found he could go an increasingly long time
without dizziness now and his conscience began to nag
him a little. He ought to go back to Fort Smith and
report for duty. He was still on the payroll; at least he
assumed he was. Fact was he had grown to like it here
and wasn't particularly eager to start toting that pistol
again. In a way this place gave him a comfortable feeling
of being home.

He knew Naomi had the most to do with it. It might
be a long time before he would chance by here again. He
had grown to like being around her.

But he decided finally there was no longer any valid
excuse for staying off of the job. He thought he could
make Fort Smith if he didn't push himself too fast.

"I reckon I'll be leavin' for town," he told the family at
supper. He was looking at Naomi when he spoke, and he

noticed that she lowered her head so he couldn't see her eyes. He tried to make light of it. "I been drawin' federal wages and not doin' any work. I reckon they could jail me for stealin'."

Elijah's heavy moustache seemed to droop. "We'll miss you, boy. Somehow you've sort of filled an empty spot that's been in this house since . . ." He let it trail off there.

Naomi finally brought herself to speak. "You shouldn't hurry yourself, Justin. You're not strong yet."

"I'm strong enough and I been a burden here too long."

Naomi said, "Papa, can't you talk to him?"

Elijah shrugged. "I'd like to, girl, but a man has got a duty. When it calls him he goes, like I went to serve in the big war. You can't hold a man back from that."

Matthew frowned, watching his sister as if he had just come to a sudden realization. "Look, deputy, one more day wouldn't make no big difference, would it?"

"I don't suppose it would if there was a good reason."

"Well, the reason is that I got to take a bunch of these fresh-broke ponies up the country. I could do it tomorrow. I'd feel better knowin' there was an extra man around while I was gone."

Justin tried to see a reason why he couldn't, though he didn't try very hard. "I don't suppose they'd fire me over just one more day." He saw Naomi lift her head a little and he decided he would stay whether they fired him or not.

Matthew was ready next morning at first light to head the string of horses out. "I'll pick up Blue Wing to help me," he said. "Ought to be home by dark." He left, going north.

Justin helped Elijah hitch his team of mules. He started to walk with him down to the cornfield where the plow had been left lying at the turnrow, but Elijah wouldn't hear of it. "You'd work yourself up to a heat and you ain't strong enough to face it. We'd have you on our hands another week. You just shade yourself, boy."

Justin shrugged and watched as Elijah walked the

team down the hoof-worn trail to the field, trace chains jingling. Justin stood on first one foot, then the other. Finally he decided he could keep occupied by saddle-soaping the harness in the barn; he had noticed a lot of it getting dry and tending to brittleness. He dragged it into the shade by the barn door and went to work. There was more of it than he had realized. Presently the women finished their chores in the house and started down toward the field, hoes in their hands, to help chop out the green corn. Justin waved and he caught the quick flash of Naomi's smile.

The harness took him the better part of the morning. Finished, he looked around for something else useful to do and decided to grease the wagon wheels. They needed it. He used the wagon jack to raise the rear axle. The big rear wheel turned out to be almost too much for him. He wasn't as strong as he figured. But he managed to lift it off.

Naomi came up from the field, walking toward the house. Seeing Justin she cut across to the barn and stood watching him a moment. "You'll have to eat dinner outside," she smiled. "You'll never get that grease off of you in time to eat in the house."

"Never could grease a wagon and keep myself clean."

"You don't have to do this, you know. You don't owe us anything."

"You been feedin' me for a week and a half."

"You wouldn't've been shot if it hadn't been for Matthew. So we owe *you*, not the other way around."

"I'd as soon be doin' somethin' like this as sleepin' in the shade. I don't take it as work." He had finished one wheel and started to lift it back into place. Naomi moved to help him, and he shook his head. "I'll get it. This ain't for a girl to do." The job left him breathless. The strain set his head to aching, and he hoped his face didn't show it. He had bitten off too much but he wouldn't admit that now. He would just go ahead and chew it.

Naomi said, "I came to fetch a jug of water down to the field. I'll bring it by here for you."

"Thanks, but I'm able to walk to the well. You better see after your folks."

Jug in hand, Naomi moved barefoot down the trail. Still breathing hard from exertion of lifting the wheel, Justin leaned against the barn door and watched her, admiring the easy grace of her walk, the gentle flip-flop of her long braids. It was easy to forget she was half Indian, and even when he thought of it it didn't make a difference to him anymore.

Well he couldn't stand here all day hypnotized by a girl. He turned to step back into the barn. A movement beyond the field caught his eye and he stopped. Squinting, he made out only a blur, obscured by the heavy green underbrush. His first thought was that Matthew was getting home a lot earlier than he had said. Half a dozen horsemen broke out into the clear at the edge of the plowed ground, and Justin knew it wasn't Matthew. He pushed away from the door, instinctively uneasy.

Elijah Tankard had the reins looped around his shoulders, his hands gripping the plowhandles. He leaned back against the reins, halting the team, and reached up to slip the reins over his head. His wife Dawn was working her hoe fifty feet from him, her back turned to the men. She saw Elijah halt and she turned to see what had caught his attention. She looked only a moment then began moving toward her husband.

Naomi had gone a hundred yards toward the field. She stopped, watching.

It could have been some of the neighbors; at the distance, Justin couldn't tell. But he sensed fear in the way Dawn moved to Elijah as if for protection. Justin reached instinctively for his pistol and remembered it was in the house. It wouldn't be any better than a slingshot at this distance anyway. He remembered that Matthew hadn't taken his rifle on the horseback trip. It was still in the house. Justin broke into a sprint.

Naomi stood watching. Justin shouted at her to come back. If she heard she ignored him. He wanted to run after her, but the first thing was to get that rifle.

Finding it was easy; Matthew had left it leaning in a corner of his room. But it was one of the old percussion cap kind, and finding caps and cartridges took a minute. Justin shoved a handful in his pocket and went out the door running.

Naomi was moving now toward her father and mother. The men had brought their horses to a halt in a semicircle and confronted Elijah and Dawn far down in the field.

"Naomi!" Justin shouted. "Come back here!"

She gave no sign that she heard him. She was running when Justin saw the puffs of dark smoke. The sounds of the shots came a second later. He saw Elijah Tankard fall. Dawn rushed at the men, swinging her hoe in fury. Two more smoke puffs rose, and she fell.

Naomi stopped. Justin heard her scream. The riders heard her too. They appeared startled for a moment. Then one spurred into a run through the corn, the horse laboring over the plowed rows.

"Naomi!" Justin shouted at the top of his voice.

She turned and started in his direction like a frightened doe. All this time Justin had been hurrying toward her. He could tell he wouldn't reach her before the horseman did. Justin painfully raised the rifle to his shoulder and fired. He didn't have the range. He saw dust kick up in the front of the horse. The rider kept pushing, confident Justin couldn't hit him.

"*Justin-n-n-n!*" Naomi screamed.

Damn an old slow rifle like this one, Justin cursed silently as he struggled to reload. He watched the horseman rapidly narrow the gap between himself and the girl. Other riders had lost interest in the farmer and his wife and also were moving across the field.

Dry-mouthed, Justin dropped to one knee to take steadier aim. He drew a bead across the silver sight that he had put on the rifle for Matthew. He tried to lick his lips but his tongue was dry. He took half a breath, held as steady as he could, then squeezed the trigger.

The horse stumbled and the rider pitched forward across its neck. Justin rushed again to reload. Naomi glanced back once and saw she was out of momentary danger, but she didn't slow. If anything she ran faster.

The rider was down only a moment. The horse struggled to its feet. The rider took a quick look, then swung back into the saddle.

I just must've creased him a little, Justin thought. *I'll do a damn sight better next time.*

He didn't have to. The wound must have been worse than the rider thought for the horse faltered and went down threshing. The horseman jumped free in time to avoid being pinned. He kicked at the down horse, trying to force it to its feet.

Naomi was in the clear. None of the other riders could catch her now. A pair stopped running and began to fire pistols at her, but at the distance they had no luck.

Justin had the rifle reloaded but held his fire, for he had scant chance of hitting anything and might need that load later. Naomi ran into his arms, crying hysterically. "To the house," he shouted. "We can't afford to get cut off out here in the open."

The rider who had chased Naomi was still kicking futilely at his horse. He was a hundred yards away but Justin thought he knew him. He looked like Quarternight.

Justin and Naomi made the house in a hurry. Naomi cried, "They killed them! They killed Mama and Papa!"

Going through the door he took a quick look back. The horsemen spurred for the house. All of a sudden the house didn't look like a good idea to him. It was too big for two people to defend against someone who really wanted in.

"Out the back door," Justin said. "Maybe they'll think we've holed up inside." He took time to grab his pistol and gunbelt and a few more cartridges for Matthew's rifle. He took Naomi's hand and they sprinted across the back yard, crouching low. A tangle of brush came up within twenty feet of the outbuildings. Justin didn't let Naomi slow until they were in the protection of it. Then he dropped to one knee, breathing hard and looking back.

He saw the horsemen gallop up to the house. A pair circled around to the back and swung down, their attention on the building.

"They didn't see us," Justin whispered. "They think we're still in there. Maybe we got a little time before they find out." But not much, he knew. The men would be tracking them shortly.

Naomi wept quietly, but their own peril did not allow her to dwell upon grief. She tugged at Justin's sleeve. "This way." She led him through the brush to a gravel bed where their tracks didn't show. They followed the dry gravel bed awhile then went out from it onto a slab of rock. She pointed toward another heavy growth of brush a few lengths away. Justin broke a branch off inside a bush where it wouldn't show and he carefully brushed out their tracks as they moved toward the heavy cover.

Behind them the men were pouring gunfire into the house. *Sooner or later*, Justin thought, *they'll rush it and they'll find out we're gone. I hope it's later and not sooner.*

Justin and the girl were climbing. Justin figured they were a mile from the house. A little later he decided it was closer to two.

The shots had stopped. *By now they know. They'll be hunting us.* But he and the girl had left little trail.

Naomi dropped to her knees, exhausted. She no longer wept, but dust had settled on her face and the dried tears had left tracks easy to see. She looked at Justin a moment, then leaned into his arms. The tears began to flow again. Justin didn't try to speak comforting words for they would be idle and of little help to her. He just held her and let her cry herself out.

When she was done with it he said, "You've acted like you know where we're goin'. *I* sure don't."

Her voice was tight. "There's a place up yonder in the hills. Not many people know about it. It's got water; it's got protection."

Her eyes widened and Justin turned. He saw a column of brown smoke.

"They've fired the house," he said.

She nodded and lay her head against his chest a minute, silent. Then she said, "The smoke'll bring the neighbors if the shootin' didn't. Then I guess Oates' men will leave."

"How do you know they was Oates' men?"

"Who else's would they be? Anyway I saw the one who tried to catch me. He was with Oates the other day."

"Quarternight," Justin said.

"He's the one. Oates sent them, all right."

A chilling realization came to him. "Quarternight probably realizes you can identify him. He can't afford to let you live."

"The neighbors'll scare them off when they come to see about the smoke."

"But Quarternight and them, they'll be huntin' for you."

"They won't find us where we're goin', not if we cover our tracks. Just a few of the Indians know about this place. Barney and Matthew and me, we used to play up there. It's where Barney went to hide after he killed that man."

"Sam Dark found him," Justin pointed out.

"Barney was still half drunk and scared. He didn't hide his trail. We'll hide ours."

They moved slower and were careful to leave no tracks. Weakness came over Justin now that the mortal urgency was past. He had to stop often and rest. Times his skull felt as if it would split open. He felt of his head, afraid the wound might be bleeding again; otherwise he didn't see how it could hurt so much. Whenever he stopped to rest he turned his left ear in the direction of the back trail, listening for any sound that would indicate pursuit. All he could hear was the wind rustling through the brush, or the humming of the warm-weather insects, or the chatter of birds disturbed by their presence.

Naomi bent over him once, where he had dropped. She put her hand to his cheek then carefully touched his forehead. "Justin, this has been too much for you."

"You see where I got any choice?"

She stared gravely. "Looks like us Tankards have brought you nothin' but trouble."

"Not you. It's been Harvey Oates. From the first, startin' with what his whiskey done to your brother, it's been Harvey Oates."

She cradled his head in her arms and her tears touched warm against his cheek. "I'm sorry for all that's happened to you, Justin. For your sake I wish you'd never come."

"I'm sorry for the way things turned out, Naomi. But I'll never be sorry that I came."

Daylight had faded when they reached the place she had told him about. It lay three quarters of the way up a mountain, a deep brush-filled header that could hide half an army. At the foot of it Naomi stepped barefoot into a tiny stream. All but exhausted Justin took off his boots and followed, carrying the boots and socks under his arm. The stream would leave no sign of their going. They moved up and up. Once they left the stream to go around a tiny waterfall and Justin brushed out the few tracks they made.

At last, most of the way to the top of the mountain, they came to the clear, gurgling spring that fed the stream and started it on its long journey down toward the Arkansas River.

"This is the place," Naomi told him. "We named it the Deerhorn Pocket. It'll take another Indian to find us here."

Justin flopped to the ground on his stomach and lay in silent misery, hiding his face from Naomi so she wouldn't know. But she did know. She lay down beside him, her head on his shoulder. Justin thought, *I ought to be the one to comfort her, not the other way around*. But all he could do was lie there.

"We got no food here," he pointed out finally. "We can last a day or two, maybe three. But we can't stay forever."

"We won't be here long. But even if we are, there's game aplenty . . . deer, squirrels . . ."

"We can't shoot it. They'd hear the shots."

"This has been an Indian campground a long, long time. Matthew and Barney left snares up here. And over yonder, wrapped up in oilskin, is a bow and a quiver of arrows that the boys kept here."

"I couldn't hit nothin' with a bow and arrow."

"I can. But likely we won't have to worry about it long. Matthew will know where we've gone. He'll come."

"How'll he know?"

"This isn't the first trouble that ever came to the Tankards or their kin. We made it up a long time ago that if any of us was to ever get in trouble we'd come to this place. That way the others would know where to look. Matthew will come."

"If they don't get him first." The moment he said it he wished he hadn't.

"Oh Justin," she cried, "they mustn't get him. They mustn't. He's all I got left."

Justin turned over on his side and took her hand. "You've got *me*, Naomi, if you want me."

She came into his arms.

VII

Sometime in the night they heard brush crackle. Horses were moving up into the header. Justin raised himself onto one elbow, roused out of an uneasy sleep. He reached for the rifle but he touched Naomi instead. He found that she was listening too, holding her breath.

"It can't be *them*," she said, but the fear in her voice made a lie of it.

Justin got to his feet, rifle in his hand. He stood uncertainly, wanting to move away but not knowing which way to go. One place was about like another.

"Maybe it's Matthew," Naomi said. "I told you he'd know where we are."

"Maybe." Justin decided to move down the header a little, toward the horses and away from the sound of the spring. Down there he could hear better and keep better track. Silently he motioned for Naomi to follow him. They moved into the darkness of the brush and walked carefully, trying not to step on a dead limb or snag a branch that might give them away. Justin stayed in front, the rifle up and ready. The blood pounded in his temples, bringing the pain back with a vengeance. When they had moved thirty or forty yards he dropped to one knee and held his breath, listening.

He heard a man's voice call, "Naomi! Naomi, you up there?"

Naomi cried out, "It's Matthew. I told you he'd come."

Justin was cautious. "You real sure it's him?"

Naomi was. She called to her brother, and his voice

came back strong with relief. "Stay where you're at, Naomi. We're comin'."

Justin and Naomi stepped down to the stream and waited. When Matthew sighted them in the pale moonlight, he swung from the saddle and came running, grabbing his sister. "Thank God. I was scared to death they'd killed you or carried you off."

Justin stood in silence, pondering the foolishness of an old notion that Indians never cried. When she could, Naomi told Matthew that Justin had saved her and that she had led him up here.

Justin said, "I was wishin' there was some way we could've got word to you. But we was afoot."

Matthew solemnly stared at him. "Wasn't nothin' you could do, except what you done. I'm glad you was here, Justin. As it is we got to go down and bury Mama and Papa. If it hadn't been for you I'd be buryin' my sister, too." Matthew shoved his hand forward. "From now on you're not a white man. You're a friend."

The young Indian Blue Wing had been riding beside Matthew and three more Indians had followed single file. These dismounted and came up, listening solemnly for what Naomi and Justin had to say. Naomi was too choked for talk so Justin told it as short as he could.

A middle-aged Indian whom Justin took for Blue Wing's father spoke gravely. "We heard shots. Pretty soon we saw smoke. When we came, the men rode away. Elijah, Dawn . . . they were both dead. We couldn't find Naomi. We thought maybe those men, they carried her away. Men like that, they like Indian girls."

Matthew pointed at his rifle in Justin's hand. "Kill any of them?"

Justin shook his head.

"A pity. Blue Wing's papa and the others, they didn't get close enough to recognize anybody. Did you?"

Justin glanced at Naomi and saw she couldn't answer. "I shot a horse out from under one of them. Naomi says he was Quarternight."

In the moonlight he could see cold fury in Matthew's face. "Quarternight. And behind him Harvey Oates.

That's three Tankards he's put in the grave. He'll never kill another one."

Justin frowned. "Don't you take any wild notions, Matthew."

"Nothin' wild about the notion *I* got." He turned to Blue Wing's father. "Charley, if it's all right with you we'll take them down to your place." Charley Wing nodded and Matthew took his sister's hands. "You'll be safe enough there. When we've buried the folks Charley can take you and hide you out among some of our people. Nobody'll find you unless you want to be found."

Fear lay in Naomi's eyes. "And where are you goin', Matthew?"

"You know. Don't try and talk me out of it, little sister. I'm the only man in the family now. It's up to me."

Justin said, "Matthew, the law . . ."

"Don't talk to me about the law. It hung my brother, but Oates and Quarternight and his kind run free. My people, my mother's people—they've always had their own law. What they had to do they just went out and done it."

Blue Wing was dispatched to Fort Smith to bring Sam Dark, but it would be a long time before Sam would get here. Not much was left of the night when the rest of the party reached Charley Wing's log cabin, and Charley's sad-eyed wife took her niece into her wide-open arms. Justin lay on a blanket on a small porch, but he slept little. Exhausted, he was nevertheless kept awake by the terrible scenes which kept running through his mind over and over again. At daylight everybody was up. Justin doubted most of them had slept much better than he had, least of all Matthew. They ate breakfast in silence, saddled their horses and hitched a team to Charley Wing's wagon for Charley's wife and two daughters and Naomi. They rode over the green hills, gathering other neighbors on their way to the gray ruins of the Tankard house.

At the edge of the clearing, a hundred yards from where the charred logs lay in a heap, Justin saw two men standing by a single large, newly dug grave. The men stood in solemn silence and watched as the horsemen and the wagons approached. They took off their hats and helped the women down. One spoke words that Justin took to be Cherokee and Naomi grasped the man's hand a moment. Justin realized that this was the minister-uncle, brother to Dawn. The uncle read from the scriptures, and when he was done a few of the Indians broke into a chant that made the hair stand on Justin's neck. Directly the service was done. Matthew spaded the first earth into the grave, then turned toward his horse. He paused a moment and spoke so quietly to his sister that Justin didn't hear the words. He saw her nod and reply as quietly. Matthew turned to Justin for a final word. "See you someday, friend." He stepped into the saddle and was gone. He carried with him the rifle with the silver sight.

Justin knew what might lie in store for Matthew. He wanted to stop him but he knew there was no way. Sick at heart he turned back to Naomi, and all words failed him.

I wish Sam Dark was here. Sam would know what to do.

It was another full day before Sam Dark arrived. With him came the tall Negro George Grider and the lanky, hard-eyed Rice Pegler. Justin was glad to see Sam and George. He wondered why Dark had brought Pegler along, feeling about the man as he did. Probably he had had to; orders from Marshal Yoes, or perhaps even from the judge. Rice Pegler knew his business.

Dark had heard the story from Blue Wing but he listened to it again from Justin. His expression became more grave as the event was recounted. A deep bitterness came into his eyes and a sadness as profound as if it had been his own family. "Where's the girl at now?"

"They taken her away from here. Hid her out among some of Charley Wing's kin. Oates' bunch can't find her."

Pegler noted Dark's emotion. "I don't see why you need to take it so personal. It's just another job. Anyway these are nothin' but Indians."

Justin said tightly, "They're people."

Pegler chewed a cud of tobacco then spat a brown stream at one of Charley's chickens. "You get along real good with these folks, Moffitt. Never would've suspicioned there was any Indian blood in you."

"There ain't."

Justin couldn't tell if Pegler meant malice or not. Probably he didn't; his words probably simply reflected his lifelong attitude toward people different from himself. He said, "Careful, then, or there might be Indian blood in your kids."

Dark said impatiently, "You got any idea whichaway Matthew went?"

"North. That's what Charley's people tell me. They tracked Quarternight and his bunch a long ways. When Matthew left here they already had the trail started for him."

"They still with him?"

Justin shook his head. "He sent them back; told them it was his place to take care of it."

Dark worried aloud. "If he catches up to Quarternight and he's by himself it's apt to be the last mistake he ever makes. Reckon you could talk some of Charley's people into ridin' along and showin' us? The more trackin' we can save the farther ahead we'll be."

Blue Wing put in, "I'll go with you. And I'll get one of my cousins who helped mark the way for Matthew."

Justin said, "Thanks, Blue. That'll sure help us."

Dark frowned. "Us, Justin, but not you. You ain't lookin' none too good. You'll stay here and rest."

"I've rested enough these last two days to do me for a lifetime. I could ride with you now plumb to hell."

"And that's about where you'd end up. You stay."

Angry, Justin squared his shoulders. "Them was good people and they was friends of mine. I'm goin'. Even if I have to take this badge off and ride as a civilian, I'm goin'."

Dark studied him a moment, surprised and weighing the possibilities of argument. "All right, but if you can't make it we'll just have to leave you where you fall."

"Any fallin' done it won't be by me."

They ate a quick meal prepared by the Wing women, then they started off in a long trot, led by Blue Wing and a cousin of Justin's age named Alvin James. It was a curiosity to Justin that most of the Indians bore English names like the ones he had heard all his life and that they spoke a brand of English not dissimilar to the kind he was used to. When he came down to analyzing it the biggest difference was in their faces. He had already found with the Tankards how quickly one could learn to disregard that.

The cousin pointed. "No use pickin' up the trail right away. We can cut across to where we put Matthew on it and save ourselves some travelin'."

"Let's be at it," said Dark. "The more time we save the more chance we got of keepin' Quarternight and his bunch from killin' that boy."

They didn't have a change of horses, so they had to protect the ones they rode. A couple of times Dark had to call the Indians down from trying to set up too hard a pace. "It's apt to be a long trail, and we can't afford to be makin' the last part of it afoot."

Blue Wing would nod agreement, but in a little while he would be pushing again, and the riders moved occasionally into a swinging lope. Sam Dark controlled the pace. He didn't let them stay at it long. Always when they slowed back to a trot impatience began bubbling in Justin. He had heard of runner Indians he was sure could have traveled faster than this afoot.

Normally tracking would have to end at dark, but because Blue Wing's cousin knew one of the forward points they were able to travel deep into the night. When at last Dark called a halt the two young Indians were still raring to keep moving. Dark firmly turned them down. "The horses need rest even if you don't. They're doin' all the travelin'."

It always surprised Justin how easily Sam Dark could make himself drop off to sleep. Knowing from long experience the importance of rest at critical times he had disciplined himself into the knack of catching sleep

wherever and for however long he could. Justin lay
awake much of the night, tossing restlessly, thinking of
the Tankards, of Naomi, of Matthew. His shoulder hurt
him, too, though he had studiously avoided letting it
show when Dark was looking.

Sometime before daylight Dark awakened him by
gently shaking him. He was careful not to touch the
wounded shoulder; Justin decided Dark probably knew
after all. "Rouse yourself from that blanket, button. We'll
have us a little coffee and cold bread and we'll be on our
way."

They had put an hour behind them before the sun
came up to light their way. They had ridden deep into
the day when they crossed a shallow stream and Alvin
James reined up. "This is as far as we got before
Matthew caught up to us. Trail's cold now, but I think if
we're careful we can follow it."

Dark nodded at the Negro. "George."

George Grider, Justin had learned, was highly re-
garded for his sharp eyes and his ability to follow the
dimmest of trails. He had patiently explained to Justin
once that the trick was to know how things were
supposed to look in nature and then find the telltale signs
of disturbance that revealed a man or a horse or
whatever it was had passed that way. He had tried to
demonstrate a couple of times when they were in Fort
Smith with a few hours to kill, but Justin had never been
able to see half the things George patiently tried to point
out to him. Justin had made up his mind that whatever
other qualifications he might have as a deputy marshal,
any difficult tracking job was out.

Justin soon decided Alvin James was a better tracker
than his cousin Blue Wing and George was perhaps even
better than Alvin. They faltered now and again on the
trail. Occasionally it was Alvin who picked up sign; more
often it was George. Between them they kept the riders
moving along in a fairly decent way.

Once the trail played out altogether at one particular
stretch. George and the Indians combed the area
without luck. George, ranging far out, spotted an Indian

cabin in a meadow and suggested they go ask if anyone
had seen Quarternight's bunch, or perhaps the lone
Matthew Tankard.

"Not you," Blue Wing said. "They won't talk to the
law; they're afraid of the badmen. But they'll talk to me
and Alvin."

The two young men rode to the cabin. Sitting back at a
respectful distance Justin watched an animated conversation between an Indian at the front of the cabin and the
two cousins on horseback. There was much movement of
hands and much pointing. Presently the pair came back.
Blue Wing reported. "He says we can probably pick up
the trail yonderways. He saw them all—Quarternight
first, then Matthew. Matthew was beginnin' to close up
on them when he passed here." He looked northward
worriedly. "If Quarternight stopped anywhere there's a
good chance Matthew's caught up by now."

Dark observed, "If he did he's probably been killed."

Blue Wing nodded. "Maybe his horse came up lame
or somethin'."

"Not likely."

"We can hope."

They cut across as the Indian had suggested and
picked up the trail. Justin could see much of it now,
despite his shortcomings as a tracker. He surmised that
Quarternight's group hadn't been riding very fast. They
probably hadn't expected pursuit of any serious nature,
for a large band of outlaws was considered safe in this
territory from everything except each other. The law
seldom traveled in groups large enough to stop them and
the natives were unlikely to challenge them. The
possibility of revenge was a cardinal point of outlaw
strength deep in the Territory. *Look the other way and
live* was the self-protective motto of people beyond easy
reach of the judge's court.

The hard, steady riding was agony to Justin. In the
first place he wasn't as strong as he had thought. The
horse's jarring trot kept sharp pains darting through his
healing shoulder. Times he couldn't keep his face from
twisting. He dropped back a little to protect himself

from Dark's sight, though he had an uncomfortable feeling that Dark knew and was simply waiting for him to give up and fall out.

The only way I'll quit is to faint, and I'm a long ways from that, he told himself stiffly. *Come night I'll still be with you, Sam Dark.*

And he was, though realistically he knew if things came to a sudden showdown he probably would be more a hazard than a help. A red haze lay before his eyes and he feared that when he tried to dismount he probably would go down on his face.

Dusk came. Justin expected Dark to call a halt but he didn't. George Grider said he couldn't see the tracks anymore. Dark replied, "It don't matter. There's a settlement up yonder a ways. I'm bettin' they was headed for it. It's been a restin' place for the outlaw breed a long time. Last year I was trailin' a man through here. When I hit town everybody in the country knew it. Come to find out a storekeeper had a system of warnin' people. Of a night he hung a lantern in a certain place at the front of the store. Of a day he ran up the flag. I was two days figurin' out that he wasn't just bein' patriotic."

It took a while in the dark to get lined out in the right direction. At length they came upon a well-marked wagon road and followed it. Justin rode along at the rear, head down, shoulder throbbing so that he wanted to cry out. He had no clear idea of time for it moved with a terrible slowness.

Lanternlight glowed downtrail and Justin straightened as he heard Dark say the settlement lay ahead. Justin managed to look a little more alive, whether he felt it or not. He sensed that Sam Dark turned in the saddle, watching him critically. Sam dropped back and waited for Justin to come up even with him. "You all right, button?"

"You hear me complainin'?" Justin's voice was raw and testy, a cover-up for the pain.

"If there's any trouble you let me and George and Rice Pegler take care of it. You'd just be in the way."

"Then how come I'm here?"

FLINT IF HE HAD TO DIE, AT LEAST IT WOULD BE ON HIS TERMS

Get a taste of the *true* West, beginning with the tale of *FLINT* FREE for 15 Days

Hunted by a relentless hired gun in the lava fields of New Mexico, Flint "*settled down to a duel of wits that might last for weeks...Surprisingly, he found himself filled with zest for the coming trial...So began the strange duel that was to end in the death of one man, perhaps two.*"

If gripping frontier adventures capture your imagination, welcome to The Louis L'Amour Collection! It's a handsome, hardcover series of thrilling sagas by the world's foremost Western authority and author.

Each novel in The Collection is a true-to-life portrait of the Old West, depicted with gritty realism and striking detail. Each is enduringly bound in rich, Sierra-brown leatherette, with padded covers and gold-embossed titles. And each may be examined and enjoyed for 15 days. FREE. You are never under any obligation; so mail the card at right today.

Now in handsome Heritage Editions

Each matching 6" x 9" volume in The Collection is bound in rich Sierra-brown leatherette, with padded covers and embossed gold title... creating an enduring family library of distinction.

SILVER CANYON·LOUIS L'AMOUR

THE DAYBREAKERS·LOUIS L'AMOUR

FLINT·LOUIS L'AMOUR

"That's what I been wonderin'."

Justin didn't see a sign showing the name of the settlement. It didn't matter; the name of a place had little to do with what happened there. He saw half a dozen buildings fronting on the road, most of them standing in darkness, for it was getting on into night. He made out a blacksmith shop and a mercantile. A lighted lantern hung in front of a building that had the word *hotel* painted across it. Except for lamps in windows of a few dwelling houses back away from the road the hotel was the only place in town that showed any real amount of light. Most folks either had gone to bed or were over at the hotel, it seemed.

It was plain that Dark new the place. He rode straight to the hotel and dismounted, stretching himself and taking a quick look around. He walked up to the window and peered, hand on his pistol. He jerked his head in a motion for Grider and Pegler to follow him. "Button, you stay out here with Blue and Alvin."

Justin eased from the saddle and leaned a moment against his horse, the weakness coming over him and threatening to make him fall. When his head cleared, he made his way haltingly to the window. Inside the front room he could see half a dozen men gathered around a table, playing cards. He remembered a couple of the faces. They had been with Oates when Dark and Justin and the Tankards had taken those two whiskey peddlers. A middle-aged Indian woman drowsed in a chair against a far wall. Justin theorized she was the hotel owner's wife; marriage to an Indian was one way many white men found a legal means of establishing business in the Territory.

The men looked up in surprise as Sam Dark walked in the door. Justin drew his pistol, figuring to back Dark from out here if trouble started. But no one gave any indication of starting it.

At length Dark said, "I'm lookin' for Quarternight."

A man Justin took to be the hotel owner pushed away from the table and stood up. "You got a warrant, marshal?"

"I got a witness that says he done murder. Now, where's he at?"

"You're a little late, marshal."

"I'll be the judge of that. Where'd he go?"

Justin took that for an idle question, because he was sure these men wouldn't willingly tell anything. To his surprise, the hotel man said, "He didn't go far; I'll show you, marshal."

He walked to the door and stepped out onto the little porch where Justin stood. He glanced at Justin and the Indians then looked back for Sam Dark. He pointed. "You can't hardly see it in the night, but the graveyard lies yonderway a couple hundred yards. That's where Quarternight went. If you want to take him with you you'll have to dig him up."

Dark stared, incredulous. "He's dead?"

"I'll lend you a shovel. Go see for yourself." The hotel man paused, waiting for the impact to soak in. "Now if you really want to be doin' somethin' worthwhile, marshal, you can go get the man that killed him."

"What happened?"

"Last night, about this time or a little later, we was all settin' there playin' cards just like we're doin' now. No sign of trouble, everybody just enjoyin' himself, old friends together talkin' about old times and havin' a harmless little game. All of a sudden this young Indian steps through the door with a big old rifle in his hands. He don't say nothin' to nobody. He just puts that rifle up against Quarternight's head before anybody has time to make a move. He pulls the trigger and blows Quarternight all over the room. You want to go back in there and look?"

Sam Dark shook his head. "Anybody do anything to this boy?"

"Nobody had time. It happened so fast Quarternight never did even see him, I don't think. Had his back to the door. After the shot, the place was full of smoke. We was fallin' out of our chairs, tryin' to find our guns. The boy went back out that door and disappeared into the night."

VIII

Sam Dark set a slow and easy pace going back to Fort Smith. Rice Pegler was impatient but Dark told him, "Justin Moffitt has been through a lot, his wound not bein' healed. I figure we ought to take it easy on him."

Pegler said, "I thought you was just givin' that Indian boy plenty of time to get in ahead of us and kill Harvey Oates."

"That," Dark said impassively, "sure would be a pity, wouldn't it?"

If such an event had been Dark's secret hope, however, he was disappointed. When after their leisurely trip they finally reached Fort Smith they found big Harvey Oates alive and considerably indignant. Beside him at his wagonyard was the large Negro who had been with him and Quarternight the morning the whiskey peddler was shot. "Huff here come and told me what happened to Quarternight. I reported it to the authorities. What I want to know is how come you-all here instead of out yonder trackin' that killer down?"

"That's a big old country," Dark said bluntly, making no effort to hide his feelings against Oates. "We figure that boy knows it like he knows the back of his hand. Findin' him is goin' to be awful hard."

"You won't find him here in my wagonyard!"

"As a matter of fact that's exactly where we expect to find him. Way we got it figured you're his next target. He knows Quarternight was just workin' for you, that Quarternight killed the Tankards under your orders."

"That's a slanderous lie against Quarternight and against me!"

But Justin could tell the idea of his own danger was not new to Oates. He had probably sensed it as soon as he heard about Quarternight. Matthew Tankard was not an ordinary settler to be frightened into quiet submission. "What're you goin' to do about it, Sam? It's the duty of the law to protect an innocent taxpayer."

"I figure the thing for us to do is to hang to you like the bark on a log. When he comes to get you we'll catch him."

Oates' eyes narrowed, for he plainly disliked having so much law that close. "I don't need for you to do that. I got Huff here and I got some other men that know how to use a gun. They'll protect me. It's your job to head that boy off before he ever gets this far."

Dark made a show of regret but his eyes betrayed a grim enjoyment of the situation. "How, Harvey? You know there's been a notorious whiskey peddler operatin' out of Fort Smith for years, sellin' his wares across the river. We never been able to catch him at it. If we can't find whole wagonloads of whiskey how can we hope to find one Indian boy?"

Oates' eyes crackled. "When're you goin' to quit accusin' me, Dark?"

"When I've put you away."

Oates' face was splotched. "I can't afford to fight with you; I got too much at stake here. But someday you'll run into somebody who won't stand still for you."

Dark's voice dropped. "If ever you feel like takin' the chance, Harvey, I'll be tickled to accommodate you."

"I got a business to run. Somebody else'll do it; I'll just watch. Might even buy you a headstone, Sam, if I'm feelin' good."

"Don't do me no favors."

"No favor. It'd be my pleasure."

Justin went with Sam Dark to the courthouse. There, sad-faced, he made a full report to Marshal Yoes and Judge Parker. The judge slumped, frowning. "I've

always been partial to the Indians," he said regretfully.
"Under the circumstances I hate to sign this warrant."

Dark asked, "Do you have to, judge? You know how
come Matthew Tankard to kill Quarternight. If anything
he ought to have a medal comin' to him. If we'd got to
Quarternight first you'd of hanged him anyway."

"In all probability." The judge pushed ponderously to
his feet and strode over to peer out the window down
upon the empty scaffold. He was silent a moment in
thought. "But that would've been a legal death, done in
full justification according to the law. What young
Tankard did was, in effect, a lynching. No matter how we
try to justify him the facts still remain. Quarternight was
as yet untried, unconvicted. That boy was his own jury,
his own executioner. The killing was murder, and he
must answer for it as such."

Justin had kept still, listening. Now he argued. "If
you'd been there like I was and seen what they done to
his father and mother, your honor, you couldn't bring
yourself to convict him."

Parker kept staring out the window. "The law is clear.
There may come a day when this court can afford to take
liberties with it, but for now if law is ever to be brought
to the Territory it must be applied as relentlessly to our
friends as to our enemies. Certainly I feel pity for that
boy. But I feel even more pity for the Territory. I cannot
afford emotion in the courtroom no matter how much of
it I have here in the privacy of these chambers. It's your
job, Mister Dark, to find that lad and bring him in. It will
be mine to give him a fair and impartial trial according to
the statutes."

Dark looked at the warrant, as yet unsigned. "I hope,
sir, that you'll let me do the job in my own way." He
explained about the likelihood that Matthew Tankard
would sooner or later come for Oates. "What I want to
do is put a full guard on Harvey Oates for his own
protection. If he sneezes I want me or somebody under
me to be close enough to wipe his nose. We been wishin'
a long time for a legal excuse to put this kind of guard on
him and now Matthew has given it to us. As long as

Matthew is out there we can stay so close to Harvey that
he can't move a pint of whiskey across that river without
us seein' it."

Judge Parker, for all his somber reputation, had a
streak of humor that let him appreciate a fine bit of irony.
"If in the process of guarding Mister Oates you should
happen to find evidence of illegal activity on his part, I
trust you would not hesitate to fetch him before this
court."

"I wouldn't hesitate a minute, your honor. I might
even rouse you from your bed."

"Mrs. Parker might complain, but for me it would be a
night's sleep well lost, Mister Dark. Whatever you need
to set up your guard you have full authority from me
through Marshal Yoes."

In the long days that followed Justin Moffitt was given
much opportunity to lie in Dark's shack and catch up on
his rest, to let his shoulder heal without complication
from undue exertion. Officially he stood regular tours of
duty, but unofficially Sam Dark relieved him from many
of these or at least cut them short. Justin argued at first,
considering this an imposition against Dark. But Dark,
moodier than ever since the deaths of the Tankards,
spent all but his eating and sleeping hours as near to
Oates as he could get, on duty or off.

That this constant attention was a hindrance to the
normal conduct of Oates' business was obvious. The first
thing Justin saw in Oates' big warehouse was a very large
store of whiskey, both bottled and in barrels. There was
nothing illegal about it so long as it remained stored here
or went into trade east of the river. But if ever a bottle of
it crossed the Arkansas going west it was contraband.
Sam Dark saw to it that a deputy marshal followed every
wagon that carried a legal consignment to any of Oates'
customers. He would watch until it was unloaded at final
destination and the wagon sent away. Within very few
days it became plain that Oates was chafing under this
surveillance.

Sam Dark pointed his thumb at the large store of
whiskey and told Justin, "We got him up a stump. You

have any idea how much money he's got tied up in all that whiskey, button? It'd bust the back end out of a bank."

Justin nodded. "Looks like enough whiskey there to pickle every farmer west of the Mississippi."

"West of the Arkansas, anyway. His legal trade on this side of the river don't amount to a hill of beans. If we can keep him boxed in long enough and he can't get his money out of this whiskey we'll bust him flatter'n a wagonsheet."

The days were long and Oates' temper was short. He was given to raving at his men and more than once he lost a teamster who stamped away in anger. A couple of times he attempted a ruse to escape surveillance by throwing Dark's deputies off of the track. Always, when he paused to look back, he found Sam Dark quietly watching him.

More than once a wagonload of whiskey slipped out in the night and came close to the river before cutting east again when it was found that a deputy was trailing along, quietly watching.

One day Harvey Oates climbed to a wagonseat and cracked a whip over a newly harnessed team, causing them to break into a run as the wagon rumbled through the gate and out of the wagonyard. Sam Dark had been standing in the gate and he stepped aside just in time to avoid being run over. Harvey Oates brought the team back around, his face colored in anger. "Almost got you, Dark, and it wouldn't of been my fault. Got so a man ain't got room to turn around without he bumps into you or one of them deputies. When're you goin' to get the hell out of my way?"

Dark knew Oates had tried to kill him. Sardonically he replied, "When that Tankard boy comes you'll be glad you have us."

"If you was to see him you'd let him kill me; *then* you'd arrest him."

"Harvey, you got no faith in your fellow man."

Justin noticed that more and more Harvey Oates was having visitors. They would come, perturbed and demanding, and Oates would lead them off out of earshot to engage in animated conversations that included a lot of arm waving and hand motions. He figured these were people who normally bought Oates' whiskey, either in the Territory or for shipment to the Territory. They were running out of stocks and came in to find out why. Justin made it a point to study their faces so he would know them if he ever came across them again. Meanwhile that whiskey sat in the warehouse, unmoving, unsold. Harvey Oates was given to fruitless pacing in his wagonyard. At every opportunity he made it a point to crowd Dark and his deputies. One deputy, slammed against a wall by a span of mules, had to be treated for a broken arm.

Oates stamped across his wheel-packed loading area as Dark showed up to relieve Justin Moffitt. "Sam Dark, I've stood for this as long as I can. You got to do somethin' about it."

"Harvey, we've never stood in the way of your business. I've given the boys orders not to bother a soul. In no way at all have we kept you from the honest pursuit of an honest trade."

"In no way have you caught that damned Indian, either."

"We will. We'll outwait him if it takes till Christmas."

Oates couldn't wait till Christmas. In these several weeks he hadn't sold enough of his whiskey stocks to buy feed for his teams. Dark told Justin, "Sooner or later he's goin' to get desperate enough to try and go around us."

One night Justin was on guard at the wagonyard with George Grider. If he had been forced to it Justin would have had to admit he spent little time watching for Matthew Tankard. Dark's attitude toward Oates had become contagious, and Justin had accepted Dark's conviction that Oates would try to get out from under some of that big store of unsold whiskey. This particular night Oates seemed more nervous than usual, if that was possible. Usually after dark he would sit in his office and slowly drain about half a bottle of his own wares. This night, so far as Justin had seen, he hadn't drunk a drop. He would walk out into the wagonyard, look around expectantly, then return to his office. Presently he would come out again.

"Mister Oates," Justin told him, "if I was you I sure wouldn't be standin' close to the lantern thataway. You never saw Matthew Tankard shoot."

Irritably Oates said, "You was sent to watch out for that Indian, not to tell me what to do."

"Your neck," Justin shrugged, and he turned away.

He moved just in time. A bullet smacked into the office wall just behind him. The sound of the shot made him jump involuntarily. His next move was to grab the lantern and hurl it across the yard. That was a mistake. Instead of going out, it smashed open, and the spilled kerosene flared, throwing dancing light across the whole space.

Harvey Oates fired into the darkness and shouted, "Yonder he goes! Get after him! He tried to kill me!"

The bullet had struck closer to Justin than to Oates, but Justin had no time or inclination to argue. He had to take Oates' word that he had seen somebody in the darkness. The lanternlight had all but blinded Justin, and he saw nothing. Oates fired again. "Damn it, he's gettin' away. Go after him!"

A couple of Oates' teamsters hurried out of the barn, guns in their hands, and Oates waved them into pursuit. Justin moved out into the darkness in the direction Oates had pointed, though he still couldn't see anybody except Oates' own men and the lanky Negro Grider. "You see him, George? Was it Matthew?"

"I seen a man for a second or two. I lost him. Reckon he must've run for the river."

Justin looked back once, and he saw Harvey Oates still standing there in the open wagonyard. It struck him as odd that the man, having been shot at, would leave himself exposed that way. Light coming through the office window behind him and the still-flickering flame from the smashed lantern made him a fair target.

The teamsters raised a great hue and cry, and they fired into the darkness. Justin could hear them holler, "There he goes!"

"I still don't see him, George."

"Neither do I."

The teamsters were yelling for the deputies to come on. "We can catch him if you'll hurry," one shouted.

In moments Sam Dark and Rice Pegler and others had joined the pursuit. Trotting along beside Dark, Justin asked, "Leave anybody to watch out for Oates?"

Dark shook his head. "They're all out here tryin' to find Matthew."

"I think somebody ought to go back. I got a feelin' about this thing. It ain't right."

"You think it's counterfeit?"

"You said yourself that Oates would try somethin' to get out from under us."

Dark stopped running. He stared at Justin in the moonlight. "Go back, button, but don't let Oates see you. Stay out of sight and watch. I'll send George Grider back directly to join you. If Oates *is* fixin' to try somethin' I want him to think he's gettin' away with it."

Justin returned to the wagonyard in a slow trot, trying to regain the breath he had lost. He found the yard dark, the office lamp out. The big warehouse doors that opened into the yard were closed. He thought for a minute that Oates and everybody had gone. But he made out a dim light barely visible beneath the wide doors. Stealthily he climbed over the plank fence, keeping his body low, and hugged the fence until he had circled the broad yard and came up against the building. Ear close to the wall he could hear thumping noises inside. He knew the sound. Somebody was loading a wagon. The voices were subdued but he recognized Oates' among the others. He heard trace chains rattle and knew the wagon was being pulled up. Another wagon was rolled into place and it too was loaded. Quietly, beneath it all, Justin heard Oates' voice saying, "Hurry it up, damn it, hurry it up!"

He moved away from the door as he saw the dim light flicker out. He shrank back into the shadows and waited for the doors to open, but they did not. He could hear a long creaking noise from the other side of the barn, then the rattle of chains and the groans of heavily laden wagons. He realized that Oates must have hidden doors built in the back side of the barn, unnoticed unless one looked carefully for them. He was taking the wagons out the back way so they never appeared in the wagonyard. It was an exit he would have to reserve for emergencies, for the heavy wagons would soon leave permanent telltale tracks.

Justin started to climb over the fence but saw a quick movement and ducked low in the shadows. He saw nothing else for a moment. Then George Grider was standing almost close enough for Justin to touch. Justin whispered, "George!"

Grider hadn't seen him, and he jumped. "Justin, boy, what you tryin' to do to me?"

"Didn't know it was you at first. They've loaded some whiskey wagons and taken them out the back."

"Let's go see."

They moved cautiously around the building, staying in the shadows. The wagons already had passed out of sight in the darkness, though Justin could hear the faint rattle of the chains. The teamsters were being very quiet, not shouting at the teams or cracking any whips. Justin saw a man shoving the big hinged doors back into place and he dropped to his knees. When the move was finished the wall looked solid. A cross plank hid the tops of the doors. Inside the hinges probably were covered with something to keep them from being noticeable. The man who had shut the doors had a branch in his hand and was brushing the wagon tracks, trying to smooth them down to a point that they would not easily be seen.

When the man had disappeared around the dark barn, Justin whispered, "George, I'll follow after them afoot if you'll go fetch our horses. I'll hang back to where you can find me."

"Reckon I ought to tell Sam Dark?"

"Later, after we know pretty well whichaway they've headed. If you took time now we might not find each other."

George Grider faded out of sight. Justin set out in a

gentle sprint after the wagons. At this point it was not difficult to follow the tracks, but he feared as soon as they turned into a public road he might lose them. He hurried along following the sounds. At length he was close enough to see the rear wagon. He had guessed there were two, but now he could tell there were three.

Mister Dark had Oates pegged right, Justin thought. *He was getting desperate to sell some whiskey.*

Justin couldn't tell whether Oates had come with the wagons. It was his best guess that Oates probably would not, for his disappearance would cause quick suspicion and possibly result in these wagons being found before they traveled a safe distance from Fort Smith. Likely Oates was hoping to get these wagons out with nobody the wiser. Chances were he had loaded them from the back side of the storage area to make the depletion of the stock less apparent to the eye.

Justin watched the wagons make a lefthand turn onto a public road. The lead wagon clumsily cut a little short, leaving a heavy set of tracks that betrayed the direction of the turn. It seemed to Justin a stupid thing to do after they had gone to all this trouble to slip out of town without being seen or heard.

In a few minutes he was reminded how green he was, for he found the thing had been done with good reason. In a wide part of the street, where wagon tracks by the hundreds were cut afresh every day, the teamsters made a complete circle and headed the teams back in the direction they had started from. Come daylight, soon as vehicular traffic started moving at its normal rate, all signs of the turn would be obliterated.

Justin decided Sam Dark would have anticipated a move like this and been ready for it; it wouldn't have surprised him as it did Justin.

The road the teamsters took led southeastward out of Fort Smith, in a direction directly opposite the normal route into the Territory. That bothered him, but he knew that if this shipment were meant for legal trade east of the state line it wouldn't have been moved out in the dark of night. Sooner or later the wagons had to turn again.

Afraid George Grider wouldn't discern the clever switch in directions, Justin waited for him at the point where the original tracks had entered the public road. When George came leading Justin's horse he saw through the teamsters' ruse and pointed his chin eastward. "Thataway?" Justin nodded, again feeling green because he knew he would have been fooled if he hadn't personally seen the wagons turn.

"You reckon they'll run yonder a little ways and then cut across the river?" he asked George.

The tall Negro shook his head. "Not right off. They ain't sure yet that they got clean away. They'll go a ways east, I expect."

The Arkansas River made a bend just above Fort Smith and then was no longer the boundary for the Territory. The wagons could cross, if they chose, without being on illegal ground. They could then bear westward and enter the Territory at a time and place of their own choosing.

Justin figured the wagons were a mile ahead of them when he swung into his saddle and trotted down the road. George Grider pulled up beside him and jerked his thumb toward the south. "We better stay off of the road. We can skirt along a ways out yonder and never get too far from it."

"Why?"

"I expect you'll see, directly."

Justin asked no more questions. He had seen enough to trust George's judgment whether he understood it or not. He also let George set the pace, which he did in a walk. It didn't make much speed, but neither did it make any sound to speak of. In a little while George reined up and cocked his head to one side, listening. He motioned Justin into a small clump of brush where they were hidden in black shadows.

A horseman came in a walk, warily scanning both sides of the road. George and Justin stepped to the ground and placed hands over their horses' nostrils to keep them from nickering. The rider went by and was soon swallowed up in the night. Justin was ready to move on, but George touched his arm and motioned for him to wait. Presently the man came back, in a trot this time and no longer looking very hard.

When he was well gone George Grider whispered, "Outrider checkin' up. Makin' sure there ain't no star-packers like us followin' along to mess things up for them. They'll go a little easier now, but I doubt they'll fall asleep. We still better give them room."

Justin and George moved into an easy trot to close the distance between them and the wagons but they didn't move back into the road. When they reached the point that they could hear the clop of hoofs and the rattle of chains they slowed to a walk again.

"They're still movin' east," Justin whispered finally. "They ain't done a thing that ain't legal."

"No use us doin' anything either, except just ride along and watch. If they don't do nothin' illegal we just had us a nice ride and plenty of fresh air."

After a while Justin thought he heard something and he raised his hand quickly. He and George both stopped. Justin stood up in the saddle to listen. George looked puzzled. "I didn't hear nothin'. Must of been the wagons."

"Wasn't in the direction of the wagons. It was out yonderway. I'd of swore I heard a horse."

He strained, but he didn't hear it anymore and George Grider's expression showed he never did hear it. Justin could tell George thought Justin had imagined it, but George was too polite to say so. "That outrider again," George suggested, "takin' him a little wider swing."

"Probably," Justin said. He didn't hear it anymore and now he was no longer positive he had heard it in the first place. He let the horse move into a walk again.

Later they both heard one sound, a rider loping away from the wagons, heading northeastward. Justin and George looked at each other, wondering and not finding any answers. A couple of hours passed and the wagons had made a few miles before the rider came back. The deputies were close enough now to see him in the moonlight. They couldn't hear the conversation but they could see him gesturing to the teamsters on the lead wagon.

Justin wondered if this might be Harvey Oates, but he returned to his earlier belief that Oates probably would stay in Fort Smith to avoid calling attention to these wagons.

Justin knew how to read time by the stars and by his judgment it was a couple of hours past midnight when the wagons left the public road, turning suddenly north on a faint trail evidently used only by farmers in the area. George Grider nodded knowingly. "They figure they're safe now. They're taking to the river."

Justin had been up this river a time or two. He knew of no ferry here and no bridge to span the Arkansas. He was curious how these freight wagons would be taken across the water. Before long he saw the full moon shimmering on the slow-moving river. "It'll be a dandy trick," he whispered, "and I'm lookin' forward to seein' them do it."

A couple of hundred yards from the point where the wagons reached the river Justin and George tied their horses. They proceeded afoot, taking their time and staying in the shadows, working their way down close enough to watch without being seen. Justin thought the men probably would lash logs against the wagon wheels on each side and float the vehicles. To his surprise he saw the teamsters were unloading their cargo. He glanced at George as if expecting an explanation, but George had none.

For the first time Justin saw a large boat tied at the river's edge. One of the freighters hoisted a whiskey keg onto his shoulder and carried it down, placing it in the boat. Then Justin knew. They weren't going to take the wagons across. Likely other wagons waited on the far side for a transfer of the whiskey. Those would make the run across into the Territory while these either went back to Fort Smith or proceeded eastward to pick up legitimate shipping elsewhere for Oates. The tracks leaving the public road would be little noticed by any but the sharpest eyes and there would be no reason to suspect there was anything wrong.

Surely, Justin thought, there must be easier ways for them than this. He doubted this was Oates' customary method of handling the trade but it was a device he could fall back upon in a tight squeeze. The beauty from Oates' viewpoint would be that if he were discovered in this transfer nothing could be proven against him. His wagons were still on legal ground.

Sure seems sometimes like they got the law stacked for the transgressor and against the poor old boy who's trying to catch him at it, Justin thought.

Moving the whiskey was a slow process for it took the boat three trips just to unload the first wagon. It started on the second wagon and Justin stretched out on the ground, taking his rest. He knew there was nothing he and George could do anyway but sit there and watch. He could make out the shape of wagons across the river. It appeared there were more of them—maybe five or six— small spring wagons of the farmer type. They would probably scatter from here like a covey of quail, hitting the Territory at several different points to make it difficult for the law to apprehend them all.

Two of us and five or six of them, Justin thought, looking helplessly at George. *Even if we split up and trail them we can't get but one apiece. That means three or four go through.*

He made out a horseman circling the place and decided they had sent the outrider again to be sure they weren't surprised. Justin had a moment of worry about their horses, tied back in the brush. But the rider didn't go near them. As Justin watched, the man tied his horse in a clump of trees and walked to the riverbank, observing from the shadows a little while, then returning to his horse and riding downriver.

Justin glanced at George and George only nodded, puzzled too. The man had walked up as if he were part of the outfit, but he hadn't joined in and hadn't stayed. For all Justin could tell it might have been Harvey Oates himself, checking up on his men, then riding on. And there wasn't anything Justin and George could do about him. Justin could respect now the frustration he had seen several times in Sam Dark.

After a while the second wagon was empty and the boat started carrying whiskey from the last one.

Going to be a lot of celebration in the Territory before long, Justin thought.

The boat was almost across with the second load out of the third wagon when George Grider touched Justin's arm and pointed across the river. Justin became aware of sudden movement among the men who had been transferring the loads there from the boat to the wagons. He couldn't make out the cause of it. Then he saw a flash and instantly heard a shot. Oates' men resting on this side of the river jumped to their feet. The men in the boat stopped rowing and the boat began to drift gently with the current. Justin saw several men on the far side come splashing out into the water. At the distance he thought their hands were raised over their heads but he couldn't tell for sure. He heard shouts but couldn't make out the words.

The men in the boat began rowing back to Justin's side of the river. Again a shot was fired and Justin knew by the sound of it that it was a heavy rifle. He thought he knew which one. It spoke a second time. The two men jumped out of the boat and started to swim. Somebody on the far bank methodically kept firing at the boat.

"George," Justin said in wonder, "he's tryin' to sink it."

"If he puts enough holes in her she'll sure enough go down," George responded. "Wonder who . . ."

The two deputies glanced at each other, and Justin knew George was reading his mind.

Matthew Tankard!

IX

The boat drifted aimlessly with the flow of the current and Matthew, across the river, was still plunking bullets into it. The boat began listing. It would sink bye and bye, carrying the load of whiskey down with it.

The shooting stopped. A flame flickered then flared into brilliance. Matthew was setting fire to the wagons.

Oates' men on this side of the river began firing random shots in Matthew's direction. Quickly shouts of protest rose up from the men Matthew had forced into the river. They were in the line of fire if any of the bullets dropped short. The firing stopped.

One after another the wagons blazed. Justin counted five. Of a sudden he began to laugh.

George Grider didn't smile. "Harvey Oates'll bust a gut when he hears about this. He ain't so rich that losin' all this won't hurt him. It'll be like bustin' both his legs. Ain't no tellin' what he might do."

"What *can* he do?"

"Put a price on that boy, for one thing. If he offers enough somebody'll fetch him Matthew Tankard's head in a sack."

"Matthew can hide out amongst the Indians."

"Even Indians—some of them—have learned that if silver jingles loud enough it'll drown out a bad conscience."

"Matthew'll take care of himself." Justin tried to sound confident, but George was raising some doubts.

George said sternly, "You know what we ought to be

doin' right now, don't you? We ought to be goin' downstream out of sight—like he done—cross over and come back up to catch him before he leaves them wagons. He's wanted by the court."

"He's a friend of mine, George."

"Man who's got a badge on his shirt and a warrant in his pocket, he ain't got no friends. He's got to see every fugitive alike. That's what that oath said, remember?"

Justin frowned. "We could pretend we never seen a thing."

"We *did* see it. We got to report it. We don't want to report we was this close to a fugitive and didn't make no try at catchin' him." George paused. "Better we catch him than for Oates to do it. That boy'd never draw another breath."

Justin thought of Matthew's face as he had seen it when his friends were burying his mother and father. He thought of the sister Naomi and wondered how he could ever face her if he took Matthew to that bleak brick prison. But he knew the Negro was right. "We'll make the effort, George."

They did, but to Justin's relief it was only an effort. By the time they swam the river and got back to the smoldering wagons, they found only the wagon men on the riverbank, cursing bitterly and swearing vengeance. They were soaking wet, all of them.

Justin and George introduced themselves as deputy marshals and asked what had happened.

One of the men swore vigorously. "Some damned Indian. He come up on us while we was busy and there wasn't a one of us could reach a gun. Halsey yonder tried, and he's got a hole in his leg. Damned Indian tried to drown us."

Justin said, "May be lucky for you it turned out thisaway. If we'd of caught you after you got to the Territory you'd of all had a long stay in Fort Smith, with expenses paid."

"Ain't no way you can prove we was goin' to the Territory."

"No reason now for us to have to. That Indian took

care of it for us." He said to George, "We'd as well be gettin' on back to Fort Smith. We got a report to make."

George's eyes accused him a little. "Ain't we goin' to trail after your friend?"

"We'd have to wait till daylight."

"That ain't long. Look in the east."

Trailing the wagons, then watching the excitement, Justin hadn't realized the night was almost gone. He had thought of the darkness as an excuse. It wasn't good enough. "All right, George, we'll wait for daylight."

It was gratifying to look at the charred wagons, their loads destroyed. Only about one boatload was left across the river and the whiskey runners couldn't risk trying to get that into the Territory now. The freighters came over from the other side to survey the wreckage in profane anger. The first light of morning showed no sign of the boat. Somewhere out there it had gone down.

A freighter eyed the deputies suspiciously. "What was you-all doin' while all this was goin' on? It's your job to help protect a man's property."

"Even if it was about to become illegal?"

"If you catch the man that done this to us I hope you let us get the first crack at him."

"Likely," said Justin, "you'll be in jail before he is."

When it was light enough George Grider began looking around for tracks. He wasn't long in finding them. Matthew had evidently made no effort to hide them. He had crossed a little way downriver. The deputies did the same and picked up his tracks without much trouble on the far side.

Justin was disappointed. "I hoped he'd head for the Territory as hard as he could run. Instead, looks to me like he went right back toward Fort Smith."

George nodded. "Didn't finish his job yet. He come after them wagons hopin' to find Oates with them. Now he's gone back to where he knows Oates is at." He was silent a minute. "I know he's your friend, but I think you better make up your mind to one thing."

"What's that?"

"You'll likely have to help bury him."

After a while it became obvious they were wasting their time fiddling along following the tracks. There could be no doubt that Matthew was heading for town. Justin and George struck up a stiff trot in a straight line.

A long time before they got there they saw the smoke. It could have been from any number of things but Justin had a feeling about it. "Matthew's a great hand with fire," he remarked. "Looks like he didn't take time to rest none."

Matthew hadn't. Justin and George found Harvey Oates' warehouse lying in piles of gray ash and heaps of black charred timbers, still smoldering, the heavy smoke rising into a cloudless summer sky. Harvey Oates paced the open wagonyard, his shirt soaked with sweat, his face begrimed from a vain battle to save his property. Sam Dark stood calmly watching him, a cold, humorless smile matching the grim satisfaction in his eyes. He looked up surprised as Justin and George rode in. "Thought you-all would be over in the Territory by now, catchin' us some fish."

George Grider let Justin tell it. Justin said, "The fish didn't make it, Mister Dark. Seems like they was crossin' the river over east a ways and they met with an accident."

Oates was suddenly interested and suspicious. "What're they talkin' about, Sam?"

Dark said, "Some wagons left your warehouse last night."

Defensively, for he plainly thought his men must have been apprehended on illegal ground, Oates declared, "Any wagons of mine that left here last night, they was stolen."

"All right," Dark conceded, "they was stolen." To Justin he said, "What happened?"

"Same thing that seems to've happened to the warehouse here. What didn't get burned got sunk with the boat, all but about enough to drown a squirrel in."

Oates' face went scarlet. "Who done it?"

Justin shrugged. "It was dark. We never seen his face."

Oates slammed a rough fist into the palm of his left hand. He turned on Sam Dark. "That same damned Indian. I tell you, Sam Dark, you better get me that Indian!"

Crisply Dark declared, "The only thing I ever want to get for you, Harvey Oates, is about six foot of good stout rope."

"You're the law . . ."

"And we'll get that boy, but it'll be for the law, Harvey, not for you. I wisht he'd caught you in your warehouse and burned you with it. A little fire like that ain't much to what you got comin' later anyway."

Oates stared into the ashes, and the misery in his face would have brought sympathy from Justin if he hadn't known the man. This loss had staggered him financially; the wound might even be mortal. Oates rubbed a hand over his face, leaving the black streaks smeared even worse. To Dark he said, "You're purposely standin' around here lettin' that Indian get away. He's over the river by now and to hell and gone."

"I ain't movin' till I hear from Rice Pegler. He was on duty here when the fire started. Ain't nobody seen him. I figure he took out after that boy. We won't know whichaway they went till we hear from Rice Pegler." He turned back to the two newly arrived deputies. "Justin, you and George better go get you some fresh horses. No tellin' when we might have to ride out of here in a hurry. And get you somethin' to eat, too. I expect you're hungry."

Justin was. He had been too excited to notice it up to now. They got the horses fed first then went to Sam Dark's shack to fix breakfast. Most restaurants in town wouldn't accept George Grider. They might let him stand guard for them against a robber but they wouldn't serve him.

Finished, they got fresh horses and rode to the federal courthouse to wait for word and to rest. They didn't rest long for Sam Dark came along directly, Harvey Oates dogging his heels. Oates was raising Hail Columbia about getting all the marshals in the Territory on the trail of that Tankard boy. Dark would have struck him if Marshal Yoes hadn't been there and if Judge Parker hadn't at one point come striding heavily down the hall. The judge glanced at Oates' agitated face and Justin thought he saw a hint of a smile tug at the ends of the jurist's graying moustache.

Presently Sam Dark had to go out to check on a rumored sighting of the Tankard boy. While Sam was gone Rice Pegler rode up to the courthouse on a winded horse that Justin knew at a glance wasn't his. It looked as if it belonged pulling a plow. Harvey Oates went trotting down the courthouse steps demanding excitedly if Pegler had caught that Indian.

Obviously tired Pegler shook his head. "Almost did," Justin heard him say as he walked out to listen. "Way yonder, the other side of the river, I caught up to him. We swapped a few shots. One of the bullets took the horse out from under me. I had to commandeer this plug off a farmer and come back for help."

Oates was anguished. "He got clean away?"

"Not clean. I put a bullet in him; I could tell that." Pegler seemed pleased with himself.

Anxiously Justin demanded, "How bad was he hurt?"

Pegler turned his attention momentarily to Justin, his eyes disapproving. "You look like you'd rather it was *him* that put a bullet in *me*."

"I asked you how hard is he hit?"

Pegler shrugged. "Couldn't tell. If it had hit him where I aimed it I'd of drug him in by his heels. One less outlaw to cost the taxpayers."

Harvey Oates said, "You're a good officer, Pegler. Wisht we had a hundred like you. Let's get you a fresh horse out of my corral, and we'll help you run that boy to the ground."

"You ain't no marshal, Oates."

"But I got horses and I got men. I'm the aggrieved party; I got a right." He paused, eyeing Pegler speculatively. "And I got somethin' else—a thousand dollars that goes to you if you nail that Indian for me. I want to hang his hide on my fence."

Pegler's jaw dropped a little. He was plainly considering it. But in a minute he shook his head. "I'm a deputy marshal in the service of the court. Ain't no thousand dollars goin' to corrupt me."

Oates stared at him. "Two thousand dollars."

That staggered Justin for he had never seen two thousand dollars. It seemed to shake Pegler, too. His tongue flicked across dry lips. He glanced at Justin, evidently wishing Justin weren't present to overhear. "Two thousand dollars." He rubbed a hand over his face and looked back at Oates. "Is that a promise?"

"Ironclad."

Pegler's hands trembled at the prospect of getting so much money at one time. But only a moment. He turned to Justin. "That boy's a friend of yours. Where do you figure he'd head now that he's got a bullet in him?"

Justin knew Oates' offer had gotten to Pegler. A cold chill ran through him at the thought of Matthew Tankard crippling along out there somewhere like some young wounded elk, this wolf pack howling on his trail. Justin had a notion where Matthew might go but he wouldn't tell Pegler. "How should I know? He's got friends all over."

Pegler frowned. "He's got a sister. Where's she at?"

That had been part of Justin's notion and it shook him that Pegler so quickly thought of it too. But Justin could honestly say, "I don't know. They hid her out for protection from Oates and his men."

Oates colored, his eyes hostile. "You and Sam Dark with your loose accusations." He jabbed a finger at Justin. "You got a duty, boy, to tell this officer everything you know."

"So he can make himself two thousand dollars?" Justin's voice was bitter.

"So I can do my duty," Pegler said stiffly. "There's a warrant out against Matthew Tankard for murder. The way you feel about him don't make no difference in your duty to help see that the law is served. You know anything, you better tell it."

Justin tensed. "All I know I told you. Anything else you got to go and find out for yourself."

"When we get back," Pegler threatened, "I'm goin' to report all this to Marshal Yoes and Judge Parker."

"You goin' to report the two thousand dollars too?"

Pegler's eyes were flinty. "With two thousand dollars in my pocket it won't matter to me whether they like it or not. I couldn't save that much in five years workin' the way I'm doin'." He turned back to Oates. "You promised me a horse. Let's be about it."

Pegler swung up onto the tired farm horse and turned in toward Oates' stables. Justin said, "I'm goin' with you, Mister Pegler."

Pegler stopped. "I don't want you, boy."

"You'll have me anyway."

"I'll tell Marshal Yoes and he'll keep you here."

"I'll tell him about the two thousand dollars and he'll peel that badge off of you."

Pegler flamed, suddenly hating Justin, but he realized he was boxed. "I'm tellin' you we got no need for you."

"Matthew Tankard is liable to have need of me. If you catch up with him I'm goin' to be there to protect him."

Pegler's voice dropped, almost inaudible. "Come, then, and be damned. But I'm warnin' you—if you get in my way I'll set you afoot." He jerked his horse angrily and turned again toward the stables.

Justin hung back. George Grider moved up gravely. "Don't you think you'd ought to wait for Mister Dark to get back?"

"I can't afford to. If they get the chance they'll kill Matthew. They'd even kill Naomi if they could get away with it. It's up to me to see they don't. You tell him to come on as quick as he can."

X

Of the eight riders the big Negro Huff took the lead, and
it was evident from the way he started that he knew
these trails well. During the days and nights the
deputies guarded Harvey Oates it had been plain to
Justin that this black man was Oates' chief bodyguard
now that Quarternight lay six feet under. Though it was
not common for white men to accept orders from a black,
Justin had noticed that when Huff spoke the Oates men
around him paused to listen. They feared him and this
was enough to offset his color. He made it a point not to
lord it over them, but he made it a point also that they
not forget who and what he was.

Justin tried to ride close enough to Pegler and Oates
that he could hear anything they said to each other.

Oates asked Pegler if they couldn't find Matthew's
tracks where he had shot the horse out from under the
deputy. Pegler nodded. "We could but there's no need.
We'd be a week trailin' him. I figure we can shortcut
him. If I was in his shape I'd want to try and get back to
home country where family or friends could take care of
me. He's got a sister out there, and other relatives. I
figure he'll go to them. All we got to do is scour the
country and we'll get him."

Justin remembered the region they rode over. The
Negro took a slightly different route from the one over
which old Elijah Tankard had led Justin and Dark. This
was understandable for Huff was probably used to the
whiskey runners' trails. He had no doubt guarded many

a wagonload of contraband making its way across these long miles of rolling hills and deep green valleys.

They rode all afternoon, pushing much harder than Justin and Dark and Elijah had pushed the time they came this direction. Whenever they reached a house or found a traveler Oates and Pegler and their five would gather close around, bristling with guns, and attempt to cow whoever they had cornered. They would demand to know if anyone had seen a wounded Indian boy, and Pegler would forcibly give the threat of taking them to the stinking cells in Fort Smith if they lied. This badgering of people brought no result, for either no one had seen Matthew or they were made of sterner stuff than Pegler thought. Pegler always left them with a final threat. "If we find out you been lyin' we'll be back thisaway."

Justin had wondered once why Sam Dark had so little respect for Rice Pegler as an officer or as a man. Justin had begun to sense the reasons weeks ago. Now he no longer harbored any doubt. Pegler gloried in power. By some accident of circumstances, no doubt, fate had decreed that he become a law officer rather than an outlaw. He could as well have been the other, Justin thought, and his manner need have been little different. There was a streak of cruelty in him that constantly sought release.

Pegler was eager for that two thousand dollars and he kept pushing Huff to set a faster pace. The Negro was inclined to give more consideration to the horses but Pegler crowded him. At times they swung into an easy lope that would carry them a quick mile, then drop back to a trot. Pegler complained when darkness came and they had to camp.

Next morning they came upon ground that had become very familiar to Justin. This was the Tankard farm. As they reached the edge of the field Justin saw Huff turn his head and glance involuntarily toward the spot where Elijah and his wife had been killed. Justin's jaw set hard. *I couldn't prove it in court, Huff, but you just settled it for me. You was here that day.* He wondered how many of the others with Oates now had also been here. Any who were had good reason to want to see the last of the Tankards dead and buried—including Naomi.

Pegler called now for a slowdown and for watchfulness. "Look out for fresh tracks," he warned. "He could be laid up here someplace drawin' a bead over his sights."

The riders spread apart, trying to watch the ground and at the same time keep a wary eye open for Matthew possibly hiding with a rifle, trapped now and determined to sell out at the highest price. They combed the field and the pastureland around it but found nothing other than a scattering of horsetracks, some of them days old. "Neighbors," Pegler grumbled. "They probably been comin' over here takin' care of things. With all them tracks how do they expect us to find the ones we're lookin' for?"

Justin had ridden in worried silence all the way from Fort Smith. He couldn't resist putting in now, "They don't. You wouldn't expect the neighbors to pitch in and help you, would you?"

Pegler gave him a hard glance but made no reply. The riders regrouped finally around the charred wreckage of the big log house. A hard smile crossed Oates' face as his gaze drifted over the cold ashes. "Whoever done this," he said, "it was a thorough job."

Justin put in again, "Like Matthew done to your wagons and your warehouse. You taught him real good, Oates."

Oates turned a shade darker. "I wasn't nowhere around when this took place, boy."

"But Huff was. And some of the others you got sittin' here."

Huff looked startled. Oates gave him a quick glance that told him to stand easy, then turned to Justin. "Loose talk can get a man killed. You have no proof. From what I've heard you was too far away to identify anybody. It was your loose talk about Quarternight that led the

Indian boy to kill him. You got Quarternight's innocent blood smeared all over your hands."

Justin could have said that Naomi could make identification, too, but he knew they were well aware of that fact. For Naomi's sake it didn't need any pushing. Justin said, "You can save the lies for people in Fort Smith ignorant enough to believe you, Oates. I know you're a whiskey runner. I know you sent Quarternight and Huff and the others to kill the Tankards. You took revenge for what happened to your peddlers and your wagons and figured to scare other people into keepin' their mouths shut."

Oates glanced at Rice Pegler. "Pegler, you better hush him up or I can't be responsible for what happens to him. There are men here with strong feelin's when it comes to bein' lied about."

Pegler fastened a hostile gaze on Justin. "You heard him, boy. You got no proof so you just keep your mouth shut."

"You know I'm tellin' the truth, Pegler. You've let the flash of that money in your eyes turn you blind. You've let them make you a party to it. They're guilty and you're lettin' it rub off on you. You won't be able to wash it away, not with two thousand dollars worth of soap."

Pegler grunted. "That's enough. I done listened to all I intend to. You've went as far with us as you're goin'."

"I'm a deputy marshal. I can go where I damn well please."

"But not with us." Pegler drew his pistol and ominously spun the cylinder. "You could have an accident. I could be checkin' my gun and let it go off and hit that horse of yours between the eyes. Then you'd be afoot and couldn't come along. Sure would be a pity to have a thing like that happen to a good horse."

Justin swallowed, for he knew Rice Pegler would do it. He might even do more if he had no witnesses or was sure of those he did have. Pegler said, "You better listen to me, boy. I'm readin' you the gospel."

"I'm listenin'."

"Then hear the rest of it. We're goin' on. We're goin'

to comb every farm in this part of the country. I figure that sooner or later, we'll find that Tankard girl. And when we find the girl we'll find the boy too."

Justin felt the blood rise to his face. "I'm bettin' you don't find either one of them. But if you do, and you hurt them any worse than they already been hurt, I'll be huntin' for you, Rice Pegler."

Pegler said stiffly, "I'll remember you threatened me, boy."

"You'd damn well better."

Justin swung to the ground to stretch his legs, and he watched in anger as Pegler and Oates and the others rode away from him, heading in the direction of the Wing house. He realized now what he should have known when they left Fort Smith—that they wouldn't tolerate him when they got into the country they were heading for, that they would do whatever was necessary to get rid of him.

Well, he thought, they wouldn't ride up on the Wing place and catch everybody asleep. Justin drew the saddlegun from its scabbard, took a firm grip on the reins and fired three shots into the air. The startled horse nearly tore his hand off and the hard jerk made pain jab through Justin's nearly healed shoulder. Justin watched the riders stop and look back at him. Oates shook his fist.

Now, Justin thought, *just try to slip up on anybody*.

He had it in mind to ride along a safe distance behind them and continue to harass them this way. But he figured this series of shots—and perhaps one more— would serve to alert the Wings. They would send somebody out, spot the riders and spread the alarm. Wherever Pegler's posse went the word would travel ahead of them.

Justin decided he could make better use of his time in another way. He let his gaze drift toward the range of hills where Deerhorn Pocket lay. He remembered what Naomi had told him about it as he and she had ridden together up there in that timbered header: "We made it up a long time ago that if any of us was to ever get in trouble we'd come to this place. That way the others would know where to look."

Up there was sanctuary. Up there was food and water, a place to hide, a place to heal. Pegler's posse, even if it should try to comb those hills, wasn't big enough to flush out a man who knew its secrets.

If Matthew had gotten this far he would have gone to the Deerhorn Pocket, Justin was convinced. No lawman knew about it except for Sam Dark, who had trailed a drunken Barney Tankard when Barney was in no condition to hide his tracks; and Justin Moffitt, who had fled here with Naomi. But even Dark and Justin probably couldn't find Matthew in the denseness of that Indian stronghold if he chose not to be found.

Justin fired three more shots in quick succession, just to insure that the Wings were well warned. Then he turned his horse toward the hills and Deerhorn Pocket.

XI

Justin wished he knew the Indian tricks about hiding his trail. George Grider had tried with little success to teach him how to find other people's trails; no one had thought to teach him about covering his own. He went about it in the most commonsense manner he could, tying the horse periodically and walking back to brush out his tracks. When he reached the creek he turned into it and rode in the water, slowly moving up the hill. He paused from time to time to look behind him. He had a nagging feeling that the posse might become suspicious and come back to watch him, but he saw no sign of that and he gradually became confident.

As he moved he watched for any sign that someone else had preceded him. If so, the tracks had been smoothed over. Increasingly he began to feel that perhaps he had guessed wrong this time; maybe Matthew hadn't headed for the pocket after all.

He found fresh horse droppings, and this renewed his earlier conviction. If Matthew Tankard hadn't gone up this hill somebody else had. Quietly, so his voice wouldn't carry back to the bottom, he began to call Matthew's name.

"Matthew, it's me, Justin. I come to help you. Matthew?"

He worked back and forth across the lower reaches of the header, stopping often to look, to listen. He kept calling. No one answered, but instinct told him he wasn't alone. He could feel another presence here in this timber, could feel eyes watching him. If he hadn't been up here before and if he hadn't established a relationship with these people, it would have been enough to spook him back down the hill. He thought he knew a little of how some early trappers and hunters must have felt, ranging out into deep and hostile Indian country. It was enough to raise the hair on the back of his neck.

He kept calling, "Matthew. You up here, Matthew?"

At length he heard a loud metallic click and involuntarily he shivered to a sudden chill. He knew the sound of a rifle hammer being cocked back. "It's me," he said shakily. "Justin. I come to help."

He saw a movement of leaves and a young man pushed his way out of the brush, rifle leveled at Justin. He recognized Matthew's cousin, Alvin James, the tracker. Alvin's eyes were not friendly. "Justin, you made a mistake comin' up here."

"I come to help."

"You still a deputy?"

Justin nodded.

"Then I don't see how you can help Matthew none. You're his enemy."

"I'm not his enemy, I'm his friend. But he's got aplenty of enemies down below that hill. I come to do what I can to see he stays out of their hands. Where's he at, Alvin?"

"If you come to take him back you just forget it."

"I won't do nothin' he don't want me to do. Take me to him."

Alvin James studied Justin a while longer before persuasion overcame suspicion. Finally, he said, "I'll take you to him, but first you shuck that gun. Any guns go up there I'll take them."

Justin pitched Alvin his gunbelt and holster, the pistol in it. Alvin looped it over his shoulder and lowered the muzzle of the rifle, using it to point. "Tie your horse then come on thisaway."

He led Justin up the side of the little stream then on across to a ledge of rocks. There beneath an overhang he saw Matthew Tankard lying on a blanket. Matthew's face was twisted and he looked weak. He was wearing an

oversized shirt somebody evidently had given him to
replace a bloodied one.

Justin asked, "How bad is it, Matthew?"

Matthew eyed him with the same suspicion Alvin
James had shown. "You askin' me as a friend or as an
officer?"

"As a friend."

"He got me in the side. Bullet went clean through,
but I bled like a stuck hog at first till I finally got it
stopped. Sure did take the vinegar out of me."

"You did good just gettin' here."

"Couldn't of done it without help."

"They're lookin' for you, you know. Harvey Oates is
headin' a posse himself, him and Rice Pegler."

Matthew's hate was plain in his blue eyes. "Oates!
Seems like every bad thing that's happened to us Oates
was behind it one way or another."

"He's offered Rice Pegler two thousand dollars to get
you and Rice has got his badge to back him up."

Matthew grimaced. "Glad to know I'm worth so much
to him. I must've damaged him worse than I thought."

"You gouged him awful deep. They figure to scour
every farm in this country lookin' for you. They're
startin' with the Wings. That's how come I fired the shots
a while ago, to stir the Wings up and have them ready."

"You fired them shots? We heard them, me and Alvin.
We figured it was the Wings or some of the others
signalin' us to lay low."

"They're not just huntin' for you, Matthew. They're
huntin' for Naomi, too. She's a witness against them. I
hope you got her hid out good."

Matthew glanced quickly at Alvin. "She *has* been.
They couldn't of found her in six months where we had
her. But now I don't know . . ."

Justin caught the sudden uneasiness and it set him
back on edge. "What do you mean?"

"We sent Blue Wing to fetch her here to help take care
of me. They're apt to be travelin' now."

Justin fretted, "She could ride right into that posse."

Matthew picked up a small stone and hurled it away in

frustration. "I told them I didn't need her but they kept after me. Said she'd want to come; you know how kinfolks are." He looked up at Alvin James. "Alvin, you better slip down off of this hill and see if you can find Naomi and Blue. Head them off before they get here."

Alvin glanced suspiciously at Justin. "I don't know about leavin' you, Matthew, him bein' one of them and all . . ."

"Go on, Alvin. I can take care of myself. You find them and get them the hell out of this part of the country, away from that posse. And don't get yourself caught."

Reluctantly Alvin agreed. "But only because Matthew says so," he told Justin, his eyes narrowed. "You do anything to hurt Matthew and I'll hunt you till hell freezes solid."

It amazed Justin how quickly Alvin disappeared. That was what made this place so good for a hideout. One moment he was there and the next he was gone, unseen and unheard. Justin knelt by Matthew. "Anything I can do to help you?"

"You've already done it, lettin' us know about that bunch of manhunters. But what about you? You're still an officer. You can't just forget you seen me up here, or can you?"

That touched on Justin's conscience. "I promised Alvin I wouldn't do nothin' you didn't want me to do. If you don't want to go in I won't force you."

"Don't that violate an oath or somethin'?"

"It does."

"How can you go on bein' an officer knowin' you've broken your oath, knowin' you had your hands on a wanted man and then let him go?"

"I don't know. I been doin' some worryin' over that."

"I sure don't figure on givin' myself up. I figure I'll lay up here till I get some strength back then I'll head west. They tell me out west I could pass for a Mexican if I learn how to talk the way they do."

"That wouldn't be your country. You wouldn't ever feel at home."

"I wouldn't feel at home on Judge Parker's gallows, that I'll guarantee."

"The judge is sympathetic to you, Matthew."

"But the law is the law. If he lives up to it and a jury finds me guilty he's got to hang me, ain't he?"

"A jury might not find you guilty."

"They'd have to. And then he'd have to hang me."

"He could give you a jail sentence if he found cause. He's let a lot of people off who've done killin', if he thought they had just cause."

"Can he guarantee me that?"

"No, I asked him. He can't make no guarantees and neither can I."

"Then I ain't goin', not of my free will."

"And I won't force you."

Matthew lay in silence a while, staring at the blue sky and at a bird soaring high. Justin wasn't sure but he thought it was an eagle. Now and again Matthew bit his lips and Justin knew he was feeling pain. In spite of it Matthew smiled. "I had to leave soon's I got the fire started in Oates' warehouse. I must've burned it good, didn't I?"

"You burned it good."

"You didn't know it, but I burned a bunch of his wagons, too."

"I knew it," Justin said. "I was there." To Matthew's look of surprise Justin explained how he and George Grider trailed the wagons, hoping to arrest the teamsters as they crossed over into forbidden ground. "You shootin' at Oates in his wagonyard gave him a chance to load them wagons and try to move them while the officers was out lookin' for you."

Matthew said, "I didn't shoot at Oates. I was there all right, waitin' for the chance to do it close enough to where I wouldn't miss. You-all was always around him, though, and I didn't get to. I figured Oates sent one of his own men out to shoot at him and lead all of you off. I stuck tight, right where I was. When the wagons went out the back of the warehouse I figured Oates was with them, so I trailed along."

Justin was nodding. "I thought so; I *did* hear you go around us."

"When they stopped at the river I took a chance and walked in amongst them while they was busy, close enough to find out Oates wasn't with them. Then I got the idea about burnin' the wagons and sinkin' the boat. So I done it. Then I went back to town and broke into the warehouse. Oates wasn't there, just a watchman. I set the warehouse afire, drug the watchman out and took off a-runnin'. But there was a marshal out there and he chased me."

"Rice Pegler."

"He was like a grassburr. I done all I could but I couldn't shake loose from him. I finally shot his horse, and that's when he put the bullet through my side."

"You was wrong to shoot Quarternight the way you done. You made another mistake when you didn't leave the country right then and there."

"I got no regrets about Quarternight. He didn't give my folks no chance; why should I give him one? The only mistake I made was in not gettin' Oates first. He was the big one, the one I really wanted. Now I may not ever get him."

"Somebody will; he won't last forever."

"Sometimes it looks like his kind *does* last forever."

Much later Alvin James came back. Justin could tell by the look on his face that something had gone badly wrong. Matthew knew too. He demanded, "What is it, Alvin?"

"I was too late, Matthew. That bunch, they already caught Naomi and Blue. They was close up and they rode onto that marshal before they knowed there was anything wrong. That marshal, he sent word to you."

"They catch you, too?"

Alvin shook his head. "No, but when I seen they had Naomi and Blue I rode in to see if they'd hurt them any. I didn't let on we was kinfolks or anything; thought I'd just play dumb. But that marshal, turned out he was one who went with us when we trailed you and Quarternight; he knowed me. He said he knowed that *I* knowed where you are. Said he'd be waitin' for you down where your house used to be. He'd have Naomi and Blue there and he'd turn them aloose if you gave yourself up. Otherwise he'd haul them to Fort Smith and throw them in prison for harborin' a fugitive. Said they could stay in there for years."

Matthew cursed. "They'd never live to Fort Smith. Oates don't want Naomi able to identify any of his men." He pushed himself to a sitting position, his hand going quickly to his side in a moment of hard pain. "Had they been mistreated any?"

Alvin glanced worriedly at Justin, then back to Matthew. He was hesitant in his answer. "Matthew, don't you do nothin' foolish."

Matthew read the answer in Alvin's oblique reply. His voice was angrily insistent. "Tell me, Alvin."

"They'd beaten Blue unconscious. I don't expect he told them nothin'."

"And Naomi?"

Alvin looked down. "She was bruised some."

Justin cursed and started in long strides down the hill. "That damned Pegler . . ."

Matthew called after him. "Justin, you come back here. You can't stop him."

"I'm a deputy marshal, same as he is."

"But you got no authority over him. And if he's got two thousand dollars at stake he'd as soon shoot you as not. Maybe rather. He could always tell them *I* done it."

Justin stopped. He hadn't seen it that way and the realization jarred him. "I'll figure out a way."

Matthew held up his hands in a sign that he wanted to be helped to his feet. "No, I'll stop him. I'll go down and give myself up. You said the judge'd be sympathetic."

"You'll never live to see the judge. They'll kill you if you go to them."

"They'll kill Naomi if I *don't* go. And maybe Blue Wing too. It looks like they've left me with no choice."

"There's bound to be somethin' else."

"If so, what? Tell me what it is."

Justin had no answer. Matthew looked gravely at him a

moment. "Justin, if you was to take me down as your prisoner, maybe *you'd* get the two thousand dollars from Harvey Oates."

"I wouldn't touch it."

"You could hire me a lawyer with it. Anyway, maybe it'd keep your friend Pegler from gettin' it."

Justin frowned, wishing there were some other way. "You sure this is what you want to do?"

"Hell no, it ain't what I want to do. But I don't see that they've given me any choice."

"Then I'll take you down and declare that you're my prisoner, under my protection. Anybody that lays a hand on you, I'll file charges."

"Don't get yourself on thin ice, Justin. They might not let you live to Fort Smith, either." Matthew tried walking but he was weak. He had to lean on Justin for support as they moved down the hill toward where his horse was hidden. When they reached the horses Matthew turned to his cousin. "Comin', Alvin?"

Alvin nodded. "I'll stay with you, Matthew."

Justin had been doing some quick thinking. "No, Alvin, you can be more help doin' somethin' else. I want you to go round up all the kinfolks you can find in a hurry. Bring them to the Tankard place. You-all can ride along with us as an escort to Fort Smith to be damn sure we all get there."

Alvin nodded, accepting the idea as a good one. "Take your time gettin' down. I'll have Tankard kin there in an hour."

But Matthew was not inclined to take his time. "They could kill Blue and Naomi while we're on our way. Let's move, Justin."

The hill was steep, and more than once Justin had to catch Matthew and hold him in the saddle. Matthew sagged, holding one hand tight against his side much of the time. His eyes glazed in fever, and his mouth hung open. "Matthew," Justin said, "you ain't goin' to make it. How about me goin' down and bringin' them here?"

"And give away this hideout? Some other Indian'll

need it someday. I don't want all the law findin' out about it."

At the bottom of the hill they rode in the creek a way, making no tracks that might lead one of the idle curious into a discovery of the Deerhorn Pocket. Their horses left a trail of water on the bank as they rode out and slanted down toward the Tankard homestead.

Matthew reeled in the saddle, and Justin rode in close to grab him. Matthew got hold of the horn, steadied himself and said, "I'll make it now. Let's go."

Justin could see the horses down by the burned-out house and barn. He could see the men gathered beneath the shady trees, waiting. He looked in vain for Naomi.

"They've seen us now," he said. "Keep your hands on the horn in plain sight so they won't have no excuse to shoot you." Justin reached down and drew the saddle-gun up from its scabbard and laid it across his lap. He made it a point to keep his horse as close as possible beside that of Matthew, preventing Matthew from being a clear and easy target. He saw a couple of the men start to move out and meet them, and Rice Pegler call them back. Pegler and Oates and the others made a ragged line as they stood forward of the trees, waiting in the sunlight. Every man had a pistol or a rifle in his hand.

Justin's blood was like ice as he looked them over one by one, trying to decide where the greatest danger lay. He took an extra long look at the Negro Huff, then at Pegler. "Rice," Justin said, "he's my prisoner."

"Our prisoner," Pegler said.

"No, mine. He's got my protection. I'll kill the first man that makes a move at him." He looked up and down the line again, making sure everybody heard him. To be certain, he repeated the threat.

Pegler gritted, "If you think you're goin' to do me out of that money . . ."

"The hell with your money!"

Justin got down cautiously, the rifle ready, his gaze taking in all the men. He stepped to Matthew's horse. "Ease down on me, Matthew." He had to shift the rifle over to his left hand and give Matthew his right arm.

Even so, Matthew went to his knees. Justin helped him to his feet, watching Pegler and Oates and the men. "He's in bad shape," Justin said.

"Good enough shape to hang him," Oates said. "Let's do it right here."

Justin pointed the rifle. "Say that one more time and I'll kill you where you stand. I got a right to protect my prisoner."

Oates swallowed, for he knew Justin meant it.

Justin heard Naomi cry, "Matthew!"

He saw her where she had been seated on the ground beneath the trees. Beside her, lying still and silent, was Blue Wing. Justin saw the blood on his clothes and he knew at a glance that Blue was unconscious. Justin glanced bitterly at Pegler. "Some of your work?"

Pegler said, "I got a right to question a prisoner."

Justin saw the marks on Naomi's face as she hurried toward her brother. "You questioned her too, I guess."

"An Indian. You always got to be a little tough on an Indian; show them you're not runnin' no bluff."

Naomi threw her arms around her brother and buried her face against his chest. When she looked up it was at Justin, and her eyes accused him. "I don't see how you could do it . . ."

Justin tried for words and didn't find them.

Matthew told her, "I asked him to bring me in. Else I was afraid they'd kill you and Blue."

Pegler heard. His eyes narrowed. "Then you knowed all along where this boy was. You wouldn't've brought him in if he hadn't wanted you to. You sold out, boy."

"If I did it was for a friend. You sold out for money."

Harvey Oates moved up and Matthew pushed his sister gently aside. Matthew said, "I'd of got you, Oates, if I'd had half a chance."

"But now," Oates taunted him. "I've got *you*."

Justin said, "Wrong. *I've* got him and you better not forget it."

"It's a long ways to Fort Smith."

Matthew's hatred overcame his caution. He lashed out at Oates. Missing, he overreached himself and went to his knees. Justin saw that Oates was drawing back his foot to kick at the boy and he stepped quickly forward, pushing the rifle at Oates. "You make one move . . ."

He was aware of sudden movement behind him. He tried to turn, but he heard a *swish-h-h*, and his head seemed to explode. He felt himself falling forward and his face struck the earth. He was aware of loud and angry voices, of Naomi's quick scream, and of a gunshot. He tried to push himself up but he couldn't find his hands. Nausea came and he knew only the blackness of a deep, deep pit, angry lights swirling in his brain. He lost all sense of time, all sense of anything except an agonizing struggle to find his hands, his feet.

When finally the nausea subsided and his eyes once more opened to a sustained level of light he found himself on hands and knees. It took a minute for him to begin to see through the clouds that seemed to have gathered around his face. He made out a shapeless mass that slowly became a man lying on the ground and a lump that became Naomi, huddled over her fallen brother.

Justin didn't have to ask. He knew. Matthew Tankard was dead. Justin tried to push to his feet but fell. He crawled on hands and knees and reached forward to touch Matthew and found no life in him. He kept reaching and found Naomi's hand and heard her begin to cry. "He's dead, Justin, he's dead."

Voices spoke to him, but it took a while for them to come clearly. He thought he knew what had happened but he asked anyway. A voice he knew was Oates' said, "You turned your back on that Indian and he tried to brain you. I shot him."

Justin kept blinking until he could see. His eyes found Pegler. "What happened, Mister Pegler?"

"Oates told you."

"I'm askin' *you*."

"And I'm sayin' Oates told you."

Naomi cried brokenly, "They're lyin'. It wasn't Matthew that hit you; it was that black man. Oates shot Matthew in cold blood."

Justin said, "You're under arrest, Oates, for murder."

Oates laughed harshly. "By whose testimony?"

"By mine."

"You didn't see nothin'. You had to ask what happened and we told you. The girl lies because he was her brother. Every man here will testify that I shot that boy to save you."

"Every man?" Trembling in anger, Justin looked again at Rice Pegler. "How about you, Mister Pegler?"

Rice Pegler looked Justin straight in the eye. "What do you think?"

A little of the nausea came again. "I think you've earned your two thousand dollars."

Justin put his arm around Naomi's shoulders and let her weep until the first anguish was drained from her. He heard horses and thought it was Alvin James coming with the Tankard kin—a little too late. Instead it was Sam Dark and George Grider. They dismounted and Sam Dark walked up silently. He stared at the lifeless Matthew Tankard, and Dark looked as if a mule had kicked him in the stomach. His voice was barely audible. "So you got him, did you, Rice?"

Pegler nodded. "Oates fired the shot, but you could say it was me that got him. Without me it wouldn't of been done."

Sam Dark bent forward and gently placed his fingers under Naomi's chin. He turned her face upward and saw the darkening bruises, the flesh beginning to swell. His voice went icy cold. "What happened to the girl?"

Stiffly Pegler said, "She gave us a little trouble, that squaw."

Sam Dark looked at Justin. "Seems like somebody gave you a little trouble, too, button."

Bitterly Justin spilled the whole story. He saw the hatred rise in Dark's face as the older deputy stared at Harvey Oates. Dark's fingers spread and stiffened as if he were choking the whiskey runner. "You and me, Harvey," he spoke finally, "seems like we don't bring these poor people anything but trouble and death."

"He was a killer."

"But you and me, we made him one. You with your rotgut whiskey, me with this badge. Well, you're through, Harvey. You're one evil that this country's had enough of. Justin says he placed you under arrest; all right, I'm takin' you in for the murder of Matthew Tankard."

Oates backed off a step, suddenly alarmed. "You got no case, Sam. Ask Pegler."

Dark turned to the tall deputy. "We been tryin' a long time to stop Harvey Oates. You ain't goin' to lie for him, Rice."

Rice Pegler tried to face Sam Dark's hard gaze. He had to look away. "Oates told you how it was, Sam."

"I also heard about that money he offered you."

Pressured, Pegler was angering. "Don't badger me, Sam."

Sam Dark stepped close enough to put his face a few inches from Pegler's. "You're a four-flusher, Rice, but I'm not lettin' you stand here and lie. I want the truth."

Pegler's face went to flame. His fist came up and struck Sam Dark beneath the chin. Dark staggered back, caught his balance and surged forward, his own fist swinging. It caught Pegler in the belly and buckled him forward.

The Negro Huff had been holding a pistol in his hand; the same pistol, Justin was sure, that had knocked him off of his feet. Huff stepped in, trying to position himself to swing it at Dark. George Grider, quick as a cat, shoved the cold muzzle of his own pistol against Huff's left ear. "Back away there," he said.

Huff turned on his heel, swinging the gun around. He stopped in his tracks at sight of George Grider's long-barreled .45. George jammed the muzzle of it against the man's front teeth, hard enough that Justin heard it connect and almost felt the pain. George held it there.

For a long moment the two black men stared at each other, each in a position to blow the other to kingdom come. But George Grider was cold as winter frost and in his eyes was something dreadful that Justin had never seen there before, something he had never suspected lay hidden behind the man's kindly face. It froze the big man Huff. The muzzle of Huff's pistol slowly sagged, and finally he let the weapon drop to the ground.

A savage smile crossed George Grider's face. He lifted his pistol, then brought it slashing down across Huff's head. The big man fell like a sack of oats.

George said, "That'll teach you about clubbin' folks."

Sam Dark and Rice Pegler were oblivious to the deadly confrontation between the two Negroes. They were pounding each other back and forth across the yard. The mutual dislike that had lain submerged for a long, long time came to the surface now. They struggled and puffed and swung their hard fists. They made little defense against each other. Each took what the other gave and tried to give better. The spectacle reminded Justin of a pair of bulls butting heads, backing away and butting again, equally strong, equally angry. Dark's face was streaked with blood, and so were his fists. Rice Pegler's shirt hung off of his shoulders in ribbons. Pegler went down first, staggered to his feet and put Dark down. They backed off at arms' length and slugged each other, and when their arms were too tired for that they closed in and jabbed fists into each other's ribs with what tiny remnant of strength was left to them. It was brutal and senseless but Justin made no move to stop it, nor did George Grider or anyone else. Justin sensed that this had been inevitable and a long time coming. When he couldn't watch anymore he shut his eyes. He could still hear the scuffling and the hard breathing. When that stopped he looked up again. The two men faced one another on hands and knees, swaying drunkenly. They fought each other to the ground.

"Rice," Sam Dark wheezed, "you're a . . . dirty . . . lyin' . . . four-flushin' . . . blood-thirsty . . ."

Rice Pegler's mouth hung open, the lips torn. "I'll get you . . . Sam Dark . . . I swear to God . . . I'll get you!"

XII

Alvin James brought the Tankard kin, half an hour too late. Appalled, outnumbering the Oates men by three to one, they seemed inclined at first to annihilate the whole bunch. Sam Dark, touching a wet cloth to his swollen face, talked them out of it. "Been killin' enough for one day. The law's slow but the law finally gets it done. That boy yonder, he wouldn't be dead today if he'd waited and let the law take its course. Sooner or later men like Harvey Oates always get caught up with. Now we got him under arrest. He'll never run loose again; for that I give you my personal guarantee."

Charley Wing looked like an angry eagle. His son was conscious now but groggy and badly beaten. "I want Oates dead," Charley said.

"The court'll do that."

"Those men . . ." Charley Wing pointed at Oates' crew, "they tell it one way. Naomi tells it another. Who will the court believe?"

"Everyone knows what these men are. The court won't believe them."

Wing's gaze shifted to the battered Rice Pegler, who sat hunched, one eye swollen shut, the other showing his hatred. Wing said, "That man, he is a deputy. He also says it as the other men say it. Will the court believe him?"

"He'll tell the truth when the time comes because he knows what *we* can tell if he don't."

Justin comforted Naomi as she laid her head on his

136

shoulder. "You got to go in with us now, Naomi," he told her. "We'll need your testimony to convict Harvey Oates." When she didn't reply he told her, "You'll have protection. There won't nobody hurt you ever again."

"I'll go, Justin. I'd take any risk now to see that he gets all he's got comin'. But do you think they'll really convict him?"

"Your word and mine against all them whiskey runners? Why wouldn't they?"

"I don't know, Justin. It's just a feelin' I got. He's been around here so long I just can't picture this country ever really bein' rid of him."

"Matthew got rid of him. He stopped him as sure as if he had shot him."

"I don't know, Justin. I'll believe it when I see it."

"You heard Mister Dark; he gave his guarantee. Now we best be goin'."

Charley Wing and many of the Tankard kin rode along as an escort to see that nothing went wrong on the way to Fort Smith. George Grider handled the team hitched to a light spring wagon borrowed from the Wings so Naomi wouldn't have to ride horseback. Keeping his horse in a walk, Sam Dark watched the girl, his face deeply sad. "She's went through an awful lot, button," he said to Justin. "She sure needs somebody now."

"She's got a lot of kin."

"That ain't what I mean."

"I know what you mean. But what kind of a life could I give her? I'd be gone the biggest part of the time workin' for the court."

"The hell with the court. You don't need it and it could get by without you."

Justin made no effort to argue with him further. Presently they began to talk about today. "What I don't understand," Dark said, "is how you found Matthew so easy. How did you know where to look for him?"

Justin told him about the Deerhorn Pocket. Dark nodded, remembering. "I never could've found Barney Tankard up there if he had been sober."

"The Indians have used it a long time," Justin said.

Dark nodded. "Beautiful. Sometimes a man needs solitude, a quiet lost place where he has time to be alone and think things through. If ever I had to run I think that's the place I'd run to."

Next day the procession came across the tumbleweed wagon lumbering along with a couple of prisoners other marshals had picked up. Sam Dark took a cold pleasure in chaining Harvey Oates ignominiously to the bed of the wagon. Harvey Oates' face flushed in outrage as the padlocks were snapped. Beside him—against Oates' protests—went Huff, for on the strength of Naomi's word he would be charged with striking Justin. George Grider would add his own charge: attempting to strike a second peace officer and threatening a third with a pistol.

Oates wheezed, "I refuse to have you drag me through the streets of Fort Smith this way, chained to the bed of a prison wagon and alongside a nigger at that."

Huff looked at him in angry surprise for Huff had been his bodyguard. The first surprise at betrayal turned slowly into a simmering hatred. Justin watched hopefully, thinking Huff might become bitter enough to turn evidence against Oates. But he reconsidered, for any testimony Huff gave against Oates would go indirectly against himself. They could expect no help from Huff.

Sam Dark rode just in front of the tumbleweed wagon, or beside it when the ground was smooth. Rice Pegler rode in the rear, well apart from Dark. George Grider was a-horseback now, and Justin drove the spring wagon and sat beside Naomi. She rode in silence most of the time, head down, her eyes closed against the sun and the dust and the ugly reminders brought by sight of the tumbleweed wagon ahead. She no longer wept for that was behind her. Justin suspected she was not thinking back so much as looking ahead.

"What'll I do when this is over, Justin? I've got no one left back there, no one to go to."

"You've got the place. The house can be rebuilt. Your friends and kin will help you with the crops. You got a fine place to live."

"But no family, Justin. I can't live there without family."

He didn't know what to tell her. The obvious answer was on his mind but he didn't want to state it.

She said it for him. "You're a farmer, Justin."

"I used to be a farmer. I'm an officer now."

"You don't have to be an officer."

"It's what I've wanted for a long time."

"Are you enjoyin' it, Justin? How did you feel about it when you went up into the Deerhorn Pocket where Matthew was? Or when you had to take him down there where those men were waitin' to kill him?"

Justin didn't answer.

She said, "There'll always be a Deerhorn Pocket of one kind or another. And there'll always be men like Matthew that you'll hate to bring down." He still didn't answer, so she went on. "It takes a certain kind of hardness to be a marshal in the Territory, Justin. I don't think you have it. You were goin' to let Matthew go free. You wouldn't've brought him down if it hadn't been for Blue Wing and me. That isn't the mark of an officer."

"Matthew was different."

"Everybody is different, in his own way. There'll be other Matthews."

The tumbleweed wagon always attracted a crowd as it rumbled through the streets of Fort Smith on its way up to the federal courthouse. Harvey Oates sat sullen and redfaced, his head down as far as it would go. He was the center of attention, for he had left here a widely known if not widely respected businessman. He had come back a prisoner chained to the wagon. Oates tried to cover his face with his arm but it didn't help. He was trembling in silent rage when the wagon pulled up in front of the courthouse to discharge the prisoners. Several deputies came hurrying out to help. Spectators' eyes were mostly on Oates as he climbed down wobbly-legged, dragging his chains. He made it a point to go ahead of the Negro Huff, whose eyes touched Oates, then turned away in resentment.

Oates wasn't in the stinking jail half an hour before a lawyer came running.

Judge Parker was conducting court, and he was not in

the habit of being disturbed for the everyday comings and goings of the tumbleweed wagon. He dispensed justice on a tightly operated schedule, starting at his regularly appointed hour each morning and staying faithfully on the bench as long as necessary to dispense with a creditable number of cases. Sometimes this took until dusk and occasionally far into the night. He was not swayed by his own fatigue or by the complaints of the hard-working attorneys who practiced before the bar. Not until late afternoon did he pause long enough to hear the report of Sam Dark and Justin Moffitt. He summoned them to his chambers and was smiling as he welcomed them. The smile dimmed at sight of Dark's battered face, and at the bandage on Justin's head.

"I was told you brought in Harvey Oates and lodged him in a cell," Parker said in his heavy voice. "They also told me the Tankard boy is dead. But nobody told me you had sustained injuries yourselves."

Dark shrugged uneasily. "Nothin' serious, your honor."

"What charge is to be brought against Oates? Selling whiskey illegally? I've waited for years to get him in front of me."

Sam Dark said, "Your honor, we're chargin' him with the murder of Matthew Tankard."

"Tankard was a fugitive," Parker reminded him.

"But not at the time he was killed. Moffitt had him under arrest and under his protection. Harvey Oates wilfully shot him in cold blood."

Parker looked quickly at Justin. "You were a witness, then?"

Justin stammered. "Well, sir . . . I didn't exactly see it myself." He touched his bandaged head. "It happened just after I got this."

Dark said, "Oates' men are goin' to swear that Matthew Tankard slugged Moffitt and that Oates shot him to protect Moffitt. But that's a lie."

"You'll need a witness."

"We have one—Matthew Tankard's sister. She's waitin' in the next room."

They brought Naomi in. Parker was dismayed at the sight of her bruises. "Did Oates and his men do this to you, young woman?"

She nodded, uneasy in the presence of this dreaded man. "Yes, sir." To his questioning she told the story as she had told it before. Judge Parker frowned. "You realize, of course, that it will be your word against all those men?"

"I'm only tellin' what's true, sir."

Parker looked at the two deputies. "It's plain these men believe you. And so do I. Now, if only the jury does . . ."

Dark's eyes narrowed. "Why wouldn't they, your honor?"

"You can never be certain about a jury."

"They *got* to hang him," Dark exclaimed. "One way and another, he's got the blood of fifty men on his hands. I gave those people out yonder my guarantee . . ."

"Never guarantee a jury." Parker placed his hands together and spread the fingers, studying them blankly. "It occurs to me that Deputy Pegler was out on the hunt for Matthew Tankard. Wasn't he there at the time this all took place?"

Justin Moffitt nodded soberly. "He was there, your honor."

"Was he a witness?"

Justin nodded again. "Yes, sir."

"Then I see no cause for concern. The word of an officer is all we'll need to see that Mister Oates never draws another free breath. Where *is* Deputy Pegler?"

Justin and Sam Dark looked at each other and Dark shrugged. It occurred to Justin that he hadn't seen Pegler since they had arrived in town. Parker strode to the door and called for Marshal Yoes.

"Yes, your honor," Yoes said. "I saw Rice Pegler. He said Sam Dark and Deputy Moffitt would take care of the written report. He asked to be assigned on another job far out in the Territory. He left an hour ago." Yoes looked narrowly at Sam Dark. "I gathered that he and Deputy Dark have had a violent disagreement. Pegler thought it would be better if he and Dark stayed out of each other's way awhile."

Judge Parker frowned at Dark. "What's the trouble between you two?"

Ill at ease Dark said, "A private matter, sir."

"Any trouble between deputies of this court can hardly be considered private, Mister Dark, if it affects the performance of their duties and the conduct of this court. I trust that in the future you and Mister Pegler will restrain yourselves."

"We'll sure try."

Parker turned to Marshal Yoes. "I don't know how soon the trial will come up for Harvey Oates but I'll want Rice Pegler here for his testimony. We can't leave anything to chance."

Yoes said, "He'll be here, sir."

Harvey Oates' attorney was in and out of the federal courthouse several times a day demanding that his client be released on bond so he could continue with the normal conduct of his business. At length Judge Parker set bond and Oates strode out of the cell and up the basement steps to sunlight and freedom. Sam Dark and Justin Moffitt stood at the top of the steps watching. Justin sensed the depth of Dark's hatred; the killing of Matthew Tankard had affected Sam more than Justin had realized at first. Perhaps it was an extension of the guilt he had felt over bringing in Barney Tankard for hanging. In a sense Dark seemed to blame himself for Matthew's death. And behind the whole melancholy chain of events had been Harvey Oates.

Dark blocked Oates' way. Oates stopped short of the top of the steps. "Move aside, Dark. I'm a free man."

"You're on bond. There's a difference. One day soon I'll get to yank you back in here. And then. . . ." he pointed at the white gallows . . . "You'll climb another set of steps. A short trip up and a shorter one down."

"Don't count on it," Oates told him.

Rice Pegler's manhunt turned into a long one. The weeks went by and little was heard from him. It suited

Justin, for with Oates' neck almost in the noose and
Pegler out of sight Sam Dark was fairly decent to live
with. He sent Justin off on a few assignments but never
any extended ones that kept him out of Fort Smith and
away from Naomi for long. They had found a family for
Naomi to stay with in town until time for the trial. As an
important prosecution witness she was given the constant protection of the court. Sam Dark gratuitously saw
to it that most of the time the duty was delegated to
Justin.

The day came for the trial and it was a relief to Justin.
After all this waiting it would be pleasant to get the thing
under way, he had thought.

He hadn't realized how wrong he could be.

The opening part was easy. The prosecution was
allowed to present its case first, and Justin was called to
give his part of the testimony building up to the death of
Matthew Tankard.

"I could tell Harvey Oates was fixin' to kick the
prisoner," Justin said as he came to the end of his
statement. "I moved to stop him. That's when Oates'
bodyguard Huff hit me over the head and Oates shot
Matthew Tankard."

At that point the complexion of the case began to
change. Oates' attorney objected strenuously to Justin's
interjecting an account of events that had occurred when
he was obviously not conscious enough to see them for
himself. Judge Parker sustained the objection. The
defense attorney came around to cross examine. He
explored Justin's relationship with the Tankard family.

"Am I to understand," he asked, "that you considered
yourself a friend of this fugitive, this Matthew Tankard?"

"I liked him," Justin admitted. "I knew him before he
was a fugitive."

"I gather from your testimony that you knew right
where to go to find him. Where was that?"

"Up in them hills."

"So all the time another duly appointed officer, Rice
Pegler, and a group of aroused citizens searched high
and low for him, you knew exactly where to find him and

you did not share that information with your fellow officer?"

Justin's fingers began nervously drumming against the arm of the witness chair. Up to now neither he nor George Grider nor Sam Dark had said anything to anyone about Oates' promise of money to Rice Pegler. This had been their ace in the hole to keep Pegler in line. Justin had been trying to avoid indicating that Pegler had any stake in the situation beyond his duty as an officer. Justin pondered his answer a while before he gave it. "I was afraid the men with Deputy Pegler wouldn't allow the prisoner to live. And they damn sure didn't."

The attorney turned quickly to Judge Parker. "Your honor, will you please caution this witness against interjecting extraneous testimony?"

Solemnly Parker admonished Justin to answer the questions only.

The attorney said, "It has become my impression that you are well acquainted with the young lady seated yonder. Who is she, Mister Moffitt?"

"Naomi Tankard."

"She is the sister of the deceased, is she not?"

"She is."

"What is the nature of your relationship with this young lady?"

"We're friends."

"Nothing more?"

Justin colored. "Nothin' more."

The attorney stared a moment at Naomi, making a show of his approval. "Quite a comely young woman, wouldn't you say? Hardly shows her Indian blood."

Judge Parker leaned forward, mouth turning downward. "Counselor, if you're trying to make a point it escapes me at this moment."

"I am on the verge of an important point, your honor."

"Well, I don't see that the young lady's Indian blood has anything to do with the matter at hand."

"I meant no disrespect, sir. I was merely trying to show that this is indeed a most handsome young woman,

one who might easily catch the fancy of a youthful
deputy marshal used to the long, lonely trails one must
ride in the performance of that type of duty. Now we've
all been his age and we're all human. I submit,
gentlemen of the jury, that a smile in the eyes of such a
girl might blind an impressionable young man like a
glance into the sun, so that he might tend to see only
that which would be favorable in her sight. I submit that
this family had a mistaken vendetta against my client and
that this girl's pleasant face and winsome smile were
used to prejudice this young officer against him."

Justin said, "Your honor, *I* object to that."

Parker shook his head and Justin knew he had erred.

Sam Dark was called, as next prosecution witness, to
describe the scene as he had come upon it after the
death. He referred to "Harvey Oates and his whiskey
runners" and brought the defense attorney angrily to his
feet. The attorney headed off any of Dark's attempted
references to Oates' whiskey trade on the basis that it
was hearsay, unproven, unfounded and purposely aimed
at prejudicing the jury.

Listening, Justin began looking nervously back toward
the door. Marshal Yoes was supposed to have had Rice
Pegler here today to testify. So far Rice hadn't been seen.

When Sam related that upon his arrival Justin had told
him about Huff clubbing him and Oates shooting Matthew, the attorney objected that this was an unsupported
statement from an unqualified witness who by his own
testimony had been suffering from a severe blow on the
head and whose knowledge of the event was limited to
what the girl had told him. On cross examination he
asked Dark if the story told by Oates and by all the other
witnesses had not varied sharply from the one told by
the girl, and if all these had not agreed upon the details.

"Them whiskey runners will all lie," Dark declared,
drawing another objection.

It had been the prosecution attorney's plan to take
testimony first from Justin, Dark and Pegler, then to
cinch the case with the emotional impact of Naomi's stark
description. But Pegler still hadn't arrived. Judge Parker

whispered instructions for deputies to go out and seek him. Meanwhile there was nothing to do but go ahead with Naomi's testimony. The prosecutor elicited from her the story she had told about the sequence of events culminating in the death of her brother while Justin sprawled unconscious. At length the defense attorney was given the right of cross examination.

He paced the floor in silence a few moments, stern gaze fixed on the nervous girl. "Young lady, would you please point out Harvey Oates to me?"

She did. The attorney asked her, "Had you ever seen him before the event you had just described?"

"Once. He came to our house with a group of men the day my father shot one of his whiskey runners." The attorney admonished her about earlier rulings on testimony of this type. "Did you—I'll broaden the question—did any of your family ever see Mister Oates sell whiskey to anyone?"

"We all knew he did it."

"You all knew, even though nobody ever saw it happen?"

"Some things people just know."

"So that your family hated him on the strength of these reports?"

"We hated him for what he done to our brother Barney."

"And exactly what was that?"

Haltingly Naomi went into the account. When the prosecutor tried to object the defense attorney pointed out that the girl herself had opened this line of testimony. Naomi told about Barney's hanging because of a crime committed when he was drunk. "It was Harvey Oates' whiskey that done it to him," she said positively.

The attorney turned to the jury. "Gentlemen, you can see the attitude of recrimination and hatred that had built up in this family, simply on the basis of an unfounded rumor, so that they were willing to go to any lengths to correct what they considered to be a woeful injustice."

"It *was* an injustice," she cried out. "He killed my

brother Barney with his whiskey. Then he sent and had my mother and father killed. And finally he killed Matthew with his own hand. I saw him do it!"

She was standing in the witness box her dark hands clenched, tears shining on her cheeks.

The attorney gave the jury time to look at her then said, "I ask you, gentlemen, if you have ever seen a woman who carried more hatred in her heart? I ask you, if she hated him so much and had a chance with one small lie to send him to the gallows would she hesitate? I submit, gentlemen, that her hatred was such that she might even have forced herself into believing she actually saw something she did not, because what she imagined suited her need for revenge. Look at her, gentlemen, and pity her. But I implore you, do not allow your pity for her to lead you into an injustice against an innocent man, my client. The testimony of our own witnesses will soon establish the real truth."

Watching first the jury then Naomi, Justin sensed that the defense had at least established some doubt in their minds.

That damned Pegler, he thought angrily, *where's he at?*

The prosecutor, all his present witnesses used up, had to plead to Judge Parker for patience. "We have one more witness whose testimony is vital to this case, your honor. He is Deputy Rice Pegler. He was supposed to be here before now, but apparently some outside duty has detained him."

"I've sent men out to hunt for him," Parker said. "When and if he arrives you can still put him on the stand. In the interests of time I suggest we proceed with the defense witnesses."

One by one the defense paraded its witnesses, who gave virtually identical testimony and who all saw clearly every move that everyone had made in those fateful moments. Not one of them had been standing in the way of the other. The defense attorney saved Harvey Oates for last and let him tell his story. It was like the others except that he could explain his motivation.

"Tankard had grabbed the deputy's pistol, you see, and

had struck him from behind. He had raised it to strike again. Now I know the next blow was sure apt to be fatal. There was nothin' else I could do, your honor, except what I done. I shot him. The way I see it I saved that deputy's life. I'm sorry he feels the way he does about me; it's the girl who done it to him. If you could've seen him the way he clung to her afterwards . . ."

The prosecutor tried to shake Oates' testimony as he had tried to shake that of the men before him. He made a dent or two but he didn't punch any holes.

The judge had called for the attorneys' summations when a slight commotion started at the back of the courtroom. Rice Pegler stood there.

Judge Parker said sternly, "Mister Pegler, you are woefully late."

"I been held up, sir."

"Are you ready to testify?"

"I suppose I'm as ready as I'll ever be, your honor."

"Then, Mister Prosecutor, I suggest you proceed with your witness."

It seemed to Justin, watching, that Pegler avoided looking at him or at Dark. In fact he avoided looking at almost everybody except, perhaps, Harvey Oates. The opening part of the questioning was similar to that given the other witnesses, establishing his presence at the scene, his reasons for being there.

"Now, Mister Pegler," the prosecutor said, "we come to the point at which Deputy Moffitt and his prisoner dismounted and moved toward you. We know from a reading of the officers' report what has been attributed to you, but we want you to describe for us in your own words the sequence of events that followed."

Pegler rubbed his hands nervously, looking at the floor. "Sir, I don't know what's in the report. I didn't write it myself; I got sent out on another assignment right away. I expect Mister Dark wrote the report." He glanced at Sam Dark then back to the floor.

"Just tell us what happened."

Rice Pegler raised his head, bringing his gaze from the floor to the ceiling then back to Harvey Oates. "What happened was that the prisoner grabbed the deputy's pistol out of his belt and hit him with it. Then Mister Oates, he shot the prisoner. That's all."

The courtroom buzzed. Justin Moffitt was on his feet. "Damn you, Rice Pegler, that's a lie!"

The judge rapped his gavel and called for order.

The prosecutor stared wide-eyed and stunned, as if Rice Pegler had struck him in the face with a shovel.

Justin shouted, "Damn you, Pegler, Oates has paid you off!"

The judge rapped again. "Mister Moffitt, if you don't sit down and be quiet I'll have to cite you for contempt. I *will* have order in this court." The judge himself was shaken and plainly disappointed. He turned to Rice Pegler. "Mister Pegler, what were you doing during this time? If you were doing your job properly it should not have been up to Mister Oates to shoot the prisoner."

"I was there, your honor. I was on the point of shootin' him myself. But Oates was closer and had a clearer shot."

The judge's face was florid. "Mister Pegler, this court has proceeded for weeks on the assumption that the material in the marshal's report was substantially the same as your own observations. If what you have just told us is true Harvey Oates should never have been arrested in the first place. Why was he?"

Pegler looked at the floor. "Me and Deputy Dark, we had us a fight over that, sir. I didn't think we ought to bring Harvey Oates in and I told Sam so. But he hated Mister Oates. He gave me a bad beatin' and he said if I crossed him he'd shoot me. So I took another assignment to get out of his way. But I made up my mind when the time come I'd be here to set things right."

Enraged, Justin glanced at Sam Dark. He found Dark hunched in his chair, his whole body trembling, his face flushed with silent fury. He made Justin think of a barrel of powder, the fuse smoking. "Mister Dark," Justin said. He didn't like what he saw in Dark's face. He feared Dark would bound across the short space to the witness

chair and grab Rice Pegler by the throat. "Mister Dark,"
Justin whispered, "don't do nothin' sudden."

Sam Dark just sat there.

It was hard to tell from the judge's face whether he
believed Pegler or not. Justin decided the judge knew
the man was lying.

But the jury didn't know it. The outcome of the case
was evident even before the attorneys went into their
final arguments. When the jury was led away to the jury
room it was gone only long enough to vote. It brought in
the inevitable verdict: not guilty.

Harvey Oates' friends in the back of the room shouted
and whooped and stomped their feet. Naomi Tankard
covered her face with a handkerchief. Sam Dark sat in a
stunned silence, trembling.

Judge Parker rapped vainly for order. He saw he
wouldn't get it. He said heavily, "Deputy Dark . . .
Deputy Pegler . . . I want to see both of you in my
chambers in five minutes!" He dismissed the court and
retreated angrily from the room.

Oates' attorney triumphantly slapped the whiskey
runner on the back, then Oates' friends began crowding
around, offering congratulations. Oates was all laughter
and smiles. Rice Pegler strode slowly across to join the
Oates group. Oates called, "Boys, you all know where to
meet me in about twenty minutes. I'll buy drinks for the
crowd." He had a special greeting for Pegler. "You timed
it just right," Justin heard him say. "I owe you somethin'."

Pegler glanced over his shoulder. "You owe me *two
thousand* somethin's."

"You'll get it."

Sam Dark had heard, too; Justin could tell by the way
he finally moved, turning his face toward Pegler and
Oates. The look in his eyes was terrible. Dark pushed
carefully to his feet and turned his back on the crowd.
He strode out of the room and down the hall.

Justin put his arm around Naomi's shoulder and led
her away. "We'd best get out of here, Naomi. This is no
place for you now."

He passed by the marshals' office and saw Sam Dark strapping on his pistol belt. "Mister Dark," Justin asked worriedly, "you goin' someplace? The judge said he wanted to see you."

"I heard him."

Oates' crowd swept down the hallway and out the wide front door shouting, laughing, pulling Oates along. Dark started for the hall then turned to look at the bewildered girl. "Honey," he said, "don't you waste any more tears. Harvey Oates has run out his string."

Sam Dark strode down the hall and out the front door. Justin called after him, "Mister Dark! Sam!" Then he followed.

He stopped at the top of the steps. Below, he saw that Harvey Oates had turned and that the crowd had spread apart a little. Oates was looking at Sam Dark, taunting him with his eyes. "What was it you was sayin' about me walkin' up them thirteen steps, Sam? Had me all but hung, didn't you, but I pulled out of it. Now it's you that's on the way out, Sam. After today there won't nobody pay any attention to you. You'll be lucky to get a job catchin' stray dogs."

"You're through, Harvey."

"Me through? I ain't even started yet."

"You've started and you've finished. You've killed your last Indian boy, Harvey."

Justin knew what was going to happen but he was powerless to move. He stood on the top step and watched as if hypnotized. Sam Dark's hand went down then came up with the pistol in it. He shoved the hand forward, thrusting the pistol almost into Harvey Oates' shirt. He fired once and he fired again.

Men shouted. Women screamed and went running in panic. But Harvey Oates never heard them. All he ever heard was that first shot.

Then, in the excitement and the frightened scurrying of the crowd, Sam Dark was gone.

XIII

Reluctantly Justin walked into the judge's office, following half a dozen other deputies. He glimpsed Rice Pegler standing halfway across the room, and for a moment Pegler stared at him, eyes bitter and challenging. Justin thought about it a little then edged toward Pegler. The tall deputy turned his face away.

Justin said, "You're not goin' after him, Pegler." He had dropped the *mister*.

Pegler stood in gray silence, trying not to hear him.

Justin said, "You lost two thousand dollars. If you want to take it out on somebody, try *me*. I'll fight you from here to the river."

Pegler still didn't answer, didn't look at him. Justin pressed. "Sam Dark called the turn on you. He called you a liar, a four-flusher. Now I'm callin' you the same. I'm sayin' Harvey Oates bought you off and hid you out till the last so nobody would have a chance to work on you, to get the truth out of you. I'm sayin' you sold us out for two thousand dollars."

Judge Parker was hunched over his desk, which was half covered by a set of warrants. He looked up in irritation. "Mister Moffitt, this has been a bad day. You're making it even worse." The shock and the strain were showing in Parker's stocky face. He looked incredibly weary, infinitely sad.

Justin moved closer. "Your honor, you're not really goin' to swear out a warrant against Sam Dark, are you? You know the kind of a man he is. You know the service he's given to this court. And you know the kind of man Harvey Oates was. You know, if the jury didn't, where the truth was in that courtroom today."

Parker gave the young deputy a long look of pity. "Mister Moffitt, you know my feelings toward Sam Dark. You also know where my duty is. This court has always stood for one thing: justice. For friend and foe alike."

"After all he's done for this court you can't send me out to hunt him down like a dog."

Parker shook his head and he made a point of extending his patience. "Not like a dog. Like a man. These marshals are his friends, most of them. They'll treat him with respect."

"But bring him in just the same, and throw him in that hellhole downstairs like any common criminal, and try him, and walk him up those thirteen steps."

"This court will do all it can for him. It will treat him fairly."

"And in the end it'll hang him."

Judge Parker shrugged, his face grave. "It might."

Justin stood in angry frustration, staring at the portly judge. Of a sudden he realized that the judge was as helpless as he, a prisoner, in a way, of his own harsh code. Justin reached up to his shirt and unpinned his badge. "I won't be a party to it, sir."

He started to place the badge on the desk but Judge Parker caught his hand and squeezed the fingers shut. "Don't act in haste, Mister Moffitt." He sat a moment that way, his hand gripping Moffitt's. He called to Marshal Yoes to clear the other men out of the room. When they were gone Parker said, "You call yourself a friend of Sam Dark's. You know that when this warrant is issued he'll be considered an outlaw. No matter how far he runs, how well he hides, sooner or later someone will find him. That someone could be a friend, like you, who will treat him with kindness and respect and pity. It could be a stranger, cold and indifferent. It might even be an enemy like Rice Pegler, who would go after him in malice."

"You'd let Pegler go?"

"There'll be a hearing for Rice Pegler, but right now there isn't time. He's still on duty. And like every other officer of this court it will be his duty to find Sam Dark if he can. I have a feeling that is one duty Rice Pegler will relish." The judge got up and slowly walked to the window, peering out upon what once had been a military parade ground. "Many a time I've stood at this window and wept for the soul of a man I had condemned to that gallows. But I've never let my feelings sway me from my duty, however harsh it might be. Sam Dark has been a man like me. He has never flinched from his duty, even when he personally hated it. His soul has known the torments of hell more than once. It's not unthinkable that in the end a man like him would have to break. But when he does he has to face the same judgment as anyone else. Better he face it at the hands of his friends."

Parker turned back around. "What I'm saying is that as a friend of Sam Dark you may have some idea where he would have gone. I'm saying that it would be far better if you went and fetched him rather than have it done by someone like Rice Pegler." He paused, his somber gaze dropping to Justin's closed hand. "You still have that badge, Mister Moffitt. What're you going to do with it?"

Justin closed his eyes a moment, then raised his hand and pinned the badge back to his shirt.

He stopped by the cabin to pack some food in a warbag and tie a blanket behind the cantle. Then he rode by the house where Naomi stayed. Her eyes were bleak as she looked at the horse. "I didn't think you'd go after him, Justin."

"I didn't intend to. But the judge made me see that I have to try. If I don't find him Rice Pegler might. Pegler would track him to China now if he had to. Better me than Pegler."

Naomi leaned to him and he held her tightly. She said, "I'll be here when you come back."

"I'll *be* back."

The Territory was big and wide and open country lay west of it all the way to the mountains and finally the

Pacific, room enough for a man to run. If Sam chose to run far Justin would have no idea where to seek him.

But in his mind was a conviction that Sam Dark would not run far. Dark was not a man to move blindly and in panic. He had always been one to study a problem through and to move with deliberation. He would hole up somewhere and survey his situation. He would think out a solid plan then act upon it.

Sam Dark knew the Territory as well as any Indian and Justin had no doubt he knew dozens of places to find security and to give him time. Justin knew only one, the Deerhorn Pocket. He realized it was a long shot but it was the only one he had. He recalled his conversations with Dark and how Dark had been taken with this hidden sanctuary deep in the Cherokee country.

"If I ever had to run," Dark said, "I think that's the place I'd run to."

This was the first mission Justin Moffitt had ridden alone in the Territory. He had wanted to bring George Grider but George had been too overcome. He could not bring himself to search for Sam Dark so he had remained in Fort Smith, on duty at the jail. "I ain't takin' the tumbleweed wagon out again," he had told Justin, "not till this is all over with. I couldn't live with myself if somebody was to bring in Sam Dark and I was to have to chain him in that wagon."

It was strange, riding alone this way. It gave Justin time and solitude in which to think and he wished it didn't, for the thoughts that kept forcing themselves upon him were no comfort. He camped on a clear-running stream and caught some fish for his supper but they had no flavor. He lay wide-eyed most of the night, staring sleeplessly at the stars. At daybreak he was up and moving.

He came at last to the Tankard place and he rode by the family cemetery above the field. A fourth mound was there now. His throat tightened as he remembered the days he had spent with these people, those last days before a smothering black blanket of tragedy fell upon them. Justin's gaze lifted then to the hills, toward the

hidden place where he might find Sam Dark. He passed
by the black ruins of the house and barn and started the
long climb.

He made no effort at covering his tracks now for he
saw no need. Either Dark was here or he wasn't. Justin
found the little stream and rode beside it letting the
horse pick its way along in a slow walk. Justin was
startled by a sound in the bushes and a buck deer
suddenly burst into sight, sprinting across in front of him
and disappearing into another thicket.

The suddenness of it unnerved him a little and he
found his hands shaking. *What am I scared of?* he asked
himself. *Sam Dark won't shoot me.*

But a nagging thought came for the first time and a
little doubt began to arise. Sam Dark had never been a
hunted man before. That could change things. Justin felt
an impulse to reach down for the saddlegun but he
quickly pushed that notion aside. *What would I do with
it if I had it? Sam Dark is a friend of mine. I couldn't
shoot him.* But that tiny worry persisted. *Maybe he
could shoot me.*

High up in the pocket he began to call for Sam Dark as
he had called for Matthew Tankard not so long ago.
"Mister Dark! It's Justin. I come to talk to you."

He rode slowly now, stopping often to rise up in the
saddle and listen. He would call then ride again.

Near the upper end of the pocket he found him. In a
tiny clearing Sam Dark suddenly appeared, rifle in his
hands. His face was lined with weariness. He seemed
somehow older, grimmer than Justin had ever seen him.
"You shouldn't of come, button."

Justin said, "Can I get down?"

Dark seemed only then to realize how he was holding
the rifle. He dropped it to arm's length at his side. "I
don't know why you'd want to, but help yourself." He
motioned with his left hand. "I got a little fire over
thisaway and a can of coffee on."

Justin tied his horse. He made a point of removing his
gunbelt and looping it over the saddlehorn so Sam Dark
would feel no threat. Then he followed Dark through the

trees to a rock overhang much like the one under which he had found Matthew Tankard. Dark had only one cup. He filled it with steaming black coffee, careful not to pour in too many grounds, and he handed it to Justin.

Dark said, "I expect things was in an uproar when you left."

Justin nodded. "They was."

"They got warrants out on me by now, I suppose."

Justin nodded again.

"You got one of them, Justin?" Dark asked.

Justin said, "I do. Everybody has."

They went silent a long time, occasionally looking at each other, most of the time looking off into space. From up here one could see for miles out across the Territory. Off in the distance Justin could see a couple of cabins and wondered idly whose they were.

At last Dark asked, "You figurin' on takin' me back?"

Justin stared into the cold and empty cup. "If you'll let me. I didn't want to come at all; the judge talked me into it. Way he said it, somebody'll get you sooner or later. He'd rather it was a friend. I don't have to tell you that you got enemies, Mister Dark."

"Rice Pegler?"

"Among others."

Sam Dark's face twisted bitterly and his knuckles went white from clenching his fists. "I figure a man could stay up here a long time and not be found. There's plenty of game to keep him from bein' hungry. I found a snare this mornin' and a cache with a bow and arrows."

"The Tankard boys!"

"The Indians around here know this place and they might figure out I was up here. But they wouldn't tell nobody. And you wouldn't tell nobody, Justin. I could stay a year if I needed to."

Justin knew better. He knew Sam Dark wasn't the kind who could live long hiding like an animal. Sooner or later he would have to come down and rejoin the human race. Even if it killed him.

"The judge said he'd give you every possible chance, Mister Dark. He said he'd see to it that you got justice."

"But in the end you know how it'd have to come out. There's been men hung on his gallows for less than what I done."

"He likes you, Mister Dark. He'll do all he can."

"If he didn't hang me he'd have to send me off to prison. That's just another kind of death. Slower, but death just the same. I've put too many men into that kind of a place. No, Justin, I won't do it."

"You're already in prison, Mister Dark, can't you see that? This place up here: it's a prison of its own if you can't leave it. Someday you *will* leave it and somebody'll kill you."

"Better a bullet than a rope or the rot of a stone cell."

Justin frowned, trying to frame his words. He had never been good at that. "The judge sent me to bring you in, Mister Dark. For your own good I got to do it."

Dark stared at him curiously. "You goin' to shoot me, Justin?"

"I couldn't do that."

"Then you're not takin' me. That's the only way you'll get me down from here. It's the only way *anybody*'ll get me down."

Justin realized then the hopelessness of it. He knew he would never persuade Sam Dark and he knew he couldn't shoot him. He pushed to his feet. "Then I reckon I'd as well be goin', Mister Dark. I'm doin' no good sittin' here—not for me and not for you."

"You just goin' to let me stay?"

"You said it yourself. I can't shoot you."

"You goin' to tell the others where I'm at?"

Justin shook his head. "You know me better than that. I won't betray you, Mister Dark."

Dark grimaced then pointed to the badge on Justin's shirt. "In that case you better shuck the badge. The minute you ride down from here without me you've violated your oath."

"The badge don't mean as much as friendship."

"That's what I'm talkin' about. When you wear that badge you got to make a choice. You're not cut out for it, Justin; I been tryin' to tell you that from the first. A man like me could do it. A man like Pegler, even. But not you, Justin; you got too much heart for it. You think I haven't got scars for the years I put into it? I got a lot more on the inside than ever show on the skin. The judge . . . he come to this country with all kinds of dreams of makin' it a fit and proper place, and he will, but he'll go to his grave grievin' over the things he had to do to change it. Stay with the job long enough and it'll kill you, button . . . your spirit, if not your body. You was born to be a farmer. Go back to it while you still can."

"This Territory is a long ways from bein' tame yet, Mister Dark. That's what I put the badge on for."

"There's other ways to tame it. The plow can do it better than the gun ever will. There'll be farmers in these hills when the outlaws and the marshals are all gone, when the judge is forgotten and the courthouse fallen down. That girl, Justin . . . do you feel about her the way I think you do?"

Justin nodded.

Dark said, "She's got land down yonder and she needs help. She can't keep it by herself. Put the badge away and go marry that girl. Love her like she was meant to be loved, and love this land, too. It'll be good to you. All that badge will bring you is grief and maybe an early grave."

Sam Dark followed Justin down to his horse. They stopped a moment and looked at each other and Dark shoved his hand forward. "Goodbye, button. Do what I said: marry that girl."

Justin nodded and turned away, reaching for the reins.

From the brush came a harsh voice that Justin knew only too well. "Raise them hands, Sam Dark! Raise them high!"

Justin whirled. Rice Pegler stepped out from behind the green foliage, letting a branch swing back with a slapping sound. He held a rifle pointed at Dark. Justin glanced at Sam Dark and saw the moment of doubt reflected in his eyes, the suspicion of betrayal. Justin cried out, "Sam, I didn't . . ."

Pegler grinned cruelly. "I followed you, Moffitt. I had a hunch you'd know where Sam was holed up and that you'd go to him, same as you did to Tankard. And I knowed when it come to the tawline that you couldn't bring him in. But *I* can bring him in. Step away from that horse, boy."

Justin measured the distance he would have to go to reach the gunbelt. Dark knew his thoughts. Dark said, "Don't try it, button. He'll kill you."

Pegler grunted. "Damn right I'd kill him. I come to fetch you in, Sam, and I'll do it dead or alive. The choice is up to you. It don't matter to me one way or the other."

Sam Dark was somber. "I told Justin and I'll tell you. I ain't goin' in to a rope."

"I don't see as you got a choice."

Sam Dark looked a long moment at Justin Moffitt, then back to Pegler. "I've got *one*," he said, and he reached for the pistol at his hip.

Pegler's rifle thundered and after it, like an echo, came the crack of the pistol. Justin's horse reared and broke loose and tried to run. Justin grabbed the reins and was dragged a few feet before he brought the horse to a stop. Dry-mouthed, heart hammering, he turned to look.

Rice Pegler sat on the ground, holding his stomach and groaning, one leg buckled under him. His hat was off. Justin tied the horse and warily moved to Pegler's side. Pegler looked up at him, his eyes begging for help. The rifle lay on the ground. Justin reached down for it, cursed bitterly and flung it away into the trees.

He walked then to Sam Dark. He knew at a glance that it was over for Dark; the rifle bullet had torn a hole in him that nobody could fix. Dark moaned as Justin tried to lift him and Justin eased him gently to the ground again. "Why did you do it, Mister Dark? Why did you do it?"

But Justin knew, though Sam Dark would never tell him. The pulse was gone; Sam Dark was dead. Justin slumped over him and broke into sobbing. When he was done and had control again he pushed awkwardly to his feet. He fetched his horse and laboriously lifted Sam

Dark into the saddle. He would carry him off the hill and see that he was buried somewhere down below, among friends.

Rice Pegler was still hunched, arms tight around his belly, his face deadly pale. He sat in a spreading pool of blood. He raised one hand, the fingers outspread, groping. His eyes pleaded. "Help me," he rasped. "Help me."

Justin Moffitt stared at him, making no move toward him.

Pegler cried out, "Help me, boy. Help me or I'll die here."

Bitterly Justin said, "Then, Goddamn you, die!" And he led the horse down the hill.

KELTON
ON
KELTON

I was born at a place called Horse Camp on the Scharbauer Cattle Company's Five Weils Ranch in Andrews County, Texas, in 1926. My father was a cowboy there, and my grandfather was the ranch foreman. My great-grandfather had come out from East Texas about 1876 with a wagon and a string of horses to become a ranchman, but he died young, leaving four small boys to grow up as cowpunchers and bronc breakers. With all that heritage I should have become a good cowboy myself, but somehow I never did, so I decided if I could not do it I would write about it.

I studied journalism at the University of Texas and became a livestock and farm reporter in San Angelo, Texas, writing fiction as a sideline to newspaper work. I have maintained the two careers in parallel more than thirty years. My fiction has been mostly about Texas, about areas whose history and people I know from long study and long personal acquaintance. I have always believed we can learn much about ourselves by studying our history, for we are the products of all that has gone before us. All history is relevant today, because the way we live—the values we believe in—are a result of molds prepared for us by our forebears a long time ago.

I was an infantryman in World War II and married an Austrian girl, Anna, I met there shortly after the war. We raised three children, all grown now and independent, proud of their mixed heritage of the Old World on one hand and the Texas frontier on the other.

Publisher's Note

Elmer Kelton won the Western Heritage Award for Best Novel for his 1987 book *The Man Who Rode Midnight*.

Elmore Leonard "should be a household name."
—The Philadelphia Inquirer

His characters become etched in your mind, his dialogue snaps off the page, and his keen understanding of the violent tensions between people who live on the edge will rivet you to your chair. Bantam offers you these exciting titles:

☐ 27099	**BOUNTY HUNTERS**	$2.95
☐ 27202	**ESCAPE FROM FIVE SHADOWS**	$2.95
☐ 27337	**GUNSIGHTS**	$2.95
☐ 27627	**GOLD COAST**	$3.95
☐ 27201	**LAW AT RANDADO**	$2.95
☐ 27097	**LAST STAND AT SABER RIVER**	$2.95
☐ 27665	**THE SWITCH**	$3.95
☐ 27098	**VALDEZ IS COMING**	$2.95

And if Western adventure is what you're after, Bantam has these tales of the frontier to offer from ELMER KELTON, one of the great Western storytellers with a special talent for capturing the fiercely independent spirit of the West:

☐ 27351	**HORSEHEAD CROSSING**	$2.95
☐ 27119	**LLANO RIVER**	$2.95
☐ 27218	**MANHUNTERS**	$2.95

- -

There was only one man who had the guts, the guns and the driving, urgent reason to buck that crew of rustlers robbing and murdering their way through the desert: Jim Lacy, alias Texas Jack, alias "Nevada."

Bantam is proud to publish the 60th Anniversary Edition of

ZANE GREY'S

"NEVADA"

Bantam has some of the best westerns available. Check to see if some of them are missing from your bookshelf.

BANTAM
SHOP-AT-HOME
C·A·T·A·L·O·G

Special Offer
Buy a Bantam Book
for only 50¢.

Now you can have Bantam's catalog filled with hundreds of titles plus take advantage of our unique and exciting bonus book offer. A special offer which gives you the opportunity to purchase a Bantam book for only 50¢. Here's how!

By ordering any five books at the regular price per order, you can also choose any other single book listed (up to a $5.95 value) for just 50¢. Some restrictions do apply, but for further details why not send for Bantam's catalog of titles today!

Just send us your name and address and we will send you a catalog!

*Coming in March 1989 . . . Elmer Kelton's
latest novel of the American West*

THE MAN WHO RODE MIDNIGHT

WINNER OF THE WESTERN HERITAGE AWARD FOR BEST WESTERN NOVEL

Here is a special preview of this exciting new book by one of the most honored authors in America, the story of a young man coming to terms with his grandfather's heritage—and with himself.

THE MAN WHO RODE MIDNIGHT
will be available in March 1989 wherever Bantam Books are sold.

Jim Ed Hendrix nervously flexed his fingers while the driver opened the baggage compartment low on the side of the bus. Jim Ed's skin prickled as he waited to retrieve his suitcase. He looked impatiently up and down the street. His grandfather was purposely letting him sweat a little, he thought.

Some wines mellowed with age. Others soured to vinegar. Wes Hendrix had always been contrary.

The sheriff moved close enough that he could have taken Jim Ed by the arm, looking at him as if he suspected he might be a pimp or a doper pusher. "Your bus'll be leavin' in a minute."

Jim Ed's stomach drew into a knot. He wished he had left that hamburger in the steamy little bus-station café where he had found it. "My grandfather's supposed to meet me here."

The sheriff frowned. "You don't look like anybody I know. Who's your granddaddy?"

Jim Ed saw a mud-streaked green pickup pull in against the curb across the street. Of a venerable age itself, it drew a four-wheel gooseneck livestock trailer from which much of the original paint had weathered away to leave the dull brown color of rust. A thin, angular old man in faded blue shirt and khaki pants stepped stiffly down into the street. He squinted against the sun and flipped away what was left of a cigarette. His gaze searched the front of the drugstore twice before it settled on Jim Ed with evident reluctance. The old man seemed to consider a moment before he hobbled across the street with a stubborn dignity that did not permit his yielding to the traffic.

Feeling a measure of relief, Jim Ed nodded in the old man's direction. "That's him."

The sheriff seemed displeased. "Wes Hendrix? You don't much favor *that* old reprobate. You must be Truman's boy." He started to turn away but paused. "Them clothes are apt to get you into a fight around here. Especially that hat. I don't like fightin' in my town." He gave Wes Hendrix a cool look, then moved on without speaking to him. The old man returned the look in kind, watching the sheriff walk into the brick-fronted drugstore. Jim Ed wondered what his grandfather had done to put himself crossways with the local constabulary.

Wes Hendrix took off a stained, misshapen rancher hat and rubbed a sleeve across his sweaty forehead. Jim Ed tensed under the pressure of unyielding gray eyes that appraised him like an unbroken colt and seemed to find him wanting. He had never been able to please his grandfather much; he had never discerned Wes's standards of excellence.

"Howdy, Tater," the old man said, finally.

Jim Ed waited in vain for Wes to offer him a hug, or even a handshake. He did not want to make the first move, so no move was made. He said, "They call me Jim Ed now."

"You used to answer to *Tater*. Was you havin' words with Wally Vincent?"

"Who?"

"The sheriff."

"He just welcomed me to town, is all."

The old man grunted, his expression saying he knew better.

Jim Ed remarked, "He didn't seem to like *your* looks any better."

"His wife inherited the ranch next to mine on the upriver side. He ain't been happy with me lately." Wes pointed his chin disapprovingly at Jim Ed's canvas bag. "Is that all the suitcase you got?"

The driver had finally set the other on the sidewalk. Jim Ed retrieved it.

Wes Henrix continued to study him critically, from the small-brimmed city hat to the T-shirt and down to the running shoes. "Reason I'm late, I had to drop a couple of calves off at the auction. I can spare the time if you want to buy yourself a decent hat."

Jim Ed's face warmed. "This one will do."

The old man frowned. "I hope you didn't pay much for it."

Jim Ed felt a rising disappointment and sense of pity. As a boy, on the rare occasions when he had seen his grandfather, he had thought him a strange, overpowering figure seven feet tall, a personification of the cowboy heroes on television. This Wes Hendrix was a wizened old man, half a head shorter than his grandson. His shoulders were bent, and his stubbled face looked more like Gabby Hayes than John Wayne. He had whisky on his breath, like the oil fielder on the bus.

Jim Ed had been given scant opportunity ever to become well acquainted with his grandfather. The few times he had visited his grandparents' little ranch during his boyhood had been largely his mother's doing, her sense of family duty and propriety overcoming the fact that an antagonism more formidable than a stone wall stood between Wes Hendrix and son Truman, Jim Ed's father. Grandmother Maudie used to visit Dallas a couple of times a year, but Wes had seldom come with her. When he did, he had paced the floor like a caged cat and always left earlier than intended. On the rare occasions when Jim Ed's father had reluctantly accompanied his family to his boyhood home, he had seemed likely to break out with hives and was grateful to see the place in his rearview mirror.

As Jim Ed studied this somber face, sun-punished and leathered and creased, he knew he had little in common with Wes Hendrix except the blood and the name.

The old man started into the street. A car's brakes groaned, but Wes continued his slow and methodical pace. Jim Ed waited for the car to move on, then proceeded around his grandfather's pickup.

He could only guess how long ago Wes had bought the vehicle, probably the last year cattle had paid a decent profit to the men who raised them. That had been a long time. The front was battered more than a little, the bumper scarred by brush and rocks and God knew what else that got in the way of a driver seventy-seven years old. Jim Ed placed the suitcase and the canvas bag in the pickup bed on top of several empty tow-sacks to which green crumbs of cottonseed feed still clung amid a settling of dust and dried, curled leaves garnered as Wes had driven across his pastures, making his own road wherever he went. Jim Ed gripped the door handle and pondered the prudence of offering to drive.

His grandfather started the engine, as if he had read the thought and rejected it. Jim Ed shoved aside a coiled rope and a bridle to make room on the seat. He had to move an assortment of stock medicine, wire pinchers and general working tools to make footroom on the floor. He bumped his head on a rifle racked against the rear window.

"What's that for?" he asked.

His grandfather replied in a gravelly voice, "You never know when you may run into a son of a bitch that needs shootin'." Wes reached down protectively to retrieve a bottle, around which a brown paper sack was tightly twisted. Jim Ed slammed the door twice before it caught; it had been sprung by some mischance suffered in the line of duty.

Wes started to pull out into the street, stopping only after an insistent honking he could not ignore. A livestock truck roared around him, trailing smoke and dust. "I'll drive," he said. "You city boys spook me."

The window was streaked where a recent light shower had tracked through the heavy layer of old dust. Jim Ed rolled it down so he could see out. He saw little that had changed since he had come from his grandmother's funeral two years ago. Like most small towns too far from the city to profit from urban employment, this one looked like last year's vine dying on the trellis. Ranches and farms were no longer enough to keep a rural town's blood pumping. There might be a couple more vacated buildings on the courthouse square; he was sure he remembered a small grocery store in a stone structure now boarded up by weathered plywood sheets. An abandoned theater's marquee threatened to slump onto the sidewalk. Ironically, a sign in the adjoining window advertised video cassettes for rent.

"Wonder the place hasn't *all* died," he commented, feeling no particular sense of loss. His few visits to the town had been mercifully short.

Wes Hendrix grunted and thrust out his left arm to signal a turn; he never had converted to directional lights. "A lot of them are holdin' on, hopin' the lake'll make them rich." He said *lake* like a cussword.

Wes Hendrix had been spare of flesh all his life, but now he looked even thinner than Jim Ed had remembered him. Like many old cowboys living in a batch camp, he probably subsisted more on black coffee than on solid food since the death of his wife. And maybe whisky, judging by his breath. The best thing that could happen to him, Jim Ed reasoned, was that he move to town and settle into a steady diet of somebody else's cooking. That was one thing about which Jim Ed's father was right.

Jim Ed said, "Dad believes they're going to condemn your ranch for the lake. He wishes you'd quit fighting and sell them the land."

His grandfather's hard knuckles bulged on the steering wheel. "When cows climb trees!"

Jim Ed said, "You could take the money and go anywhere you want to."

"I'm *already* where I want to be. I spent the first thirty years of my life huntin' that place. I ain't got thirty left to find me another one like it. If your daddy sent you here to lecture me, I'd just as well put you back on the bus."

That would have suited Jim Ed except that at the moment he had nowhere to go. He lacked the money to follow Jack and David on that promised trip to Europe. He could not return to Dallas for a while, not after the blowup that had resulted from his final-semester failure. The row had culminated in an ultimatum from his father. He lowered his voice. "I haven't said a word."

Wes grunted, glancing uneasily at him. "I tried to tell your daddy I'm no invalid. I don't need your help."

Jim Ed thought he wouldn't *be* much help.

Wes said, "Time you've dug a hundred postholes and put horsetracks all over the pastures, you'll wisht you was back in Dallas."

The Hendrix ranch lay nine miles east of town. A state farm-to-market asphalt pavement labored over, through and around the cedar-fringed hills, spending three miles to gain two. Now and again Jim Ed glimpsed the sparkling river, born of a thousand tiny springs that seeped and trickled and bubbled between flat seams of gray limestone layers deposited in the beds of ancient seas, later ripped and torn asunder by rumblings and spasms and upheavals in the earth's restless crust. The river's gift of life had drawn wild animals of infinite variety, making it a hunting ground for uncountable generations of warrior tribes who had battled to gain supremacy, mixing their blood with its clear cold waters. One after another had held dominance for a time, then was forced to yield to someone stronger in a long succession of violent displacements. The white man had come, finally, driving away the last of the bronzed warriors, then fighting one another for the right to this river and the bounties of the land around it. Sheepman had fought cattleman, and both had resisted the farmer. The faces changed, the voices changed, but always there was the river, and the struggle to own it.

Wes Hendrix's gateway was plain, no sign to mark it, nothing bearing his name except a mailbox mounted on a cedar post at the edge of the road. He stopped the pickup and waited for the dust to pass. "Tater, I wisht you'd see if I got any mail."

Jim Ed knew it was useless to tell him he had disliked the nickname *Tater* even as a boy. Stepping out of the pickup, he was a little shaken by the mailbox. Though it still bore a shiny silver newness, it was punctured by perhaps a dozen bulletholes. Inside, he found a couple of newspapers, a bill and a handful of junk mail. He closed the box, scratching his finger on a sharp edge left by a lead slug passing through.

Climbing back into the pickup, he dropped the mail on the seat and sucked the little ruby of blood which formed atop the scratch. His concern was genuine. "They may shoot at *you* next, and not just your mailbox."

Wes shook his head and set the pickup bumping across the cattleguard onto a ranch road packed hard with that ubiquitous Texas surfacing material, caliche, which seemed to underlie much of the state's topsoil. "Kids, is all. Their folks cuss old Wes Hendrix, so the kids think it's all right. I don't get my innards into an uproar over somethin' as triflin' as a mailbox."

A quarter mile from the pavement, Wes turned off to the left, onto a twin-rut road worn into the turf by years of driving over the same tracks. Jim Ed had to grip the inside door handle to avoid being bounced out of his seat. He grabbed the mail as it pitched toward the floorboard. Wes bullied the vehicle up a steep grade and stopped on a barren limestone slab atop a rocky hill.

"Git out, Tater." The voice was too stern for Jim Ed to question why. Wes pushed his door open and hobbled stiff-legged beside him to the rimrock. He pointed. "Looky yonder. I want you to see why I'm not lettin' them take this place without they put up a fight. Ever see such a pretty sight in your life?"

Jim Ed blinked. All he could see was the side of the hill, layer stacked upon layer of limestone, steeper even than the side by which they had climbed. A remnant of spring bluebonnets still showed in spots where the sheep or goats had not yet found them, and the faded red and yellow of Indian paintbrushes was scattered like the liver splotches on Wes's hands. Cedar trees had invaded most of the way to the top of the hill. Down below, liveoaks grew in dark green mottes, almost black, and beyond them a line of towering native pecan trees marked the river's course. Heavy foliage hid the water from view. As scenery, he considered it a long way from the Alps. He refrained from giving voice to the thought. "Nice," he said, wanting to be kind. He knew instantly that it was not enough.

Wes gave him a glance that spoke both of anger and despair, then hobbled back toward the pickup. He peeled the paper sack down from the neck of the bottle and took a drink, then kept his silence as he drove.

The road labored over a steep hill before pitching down toward the little headquarters. Jim Ed saw the old frame house dwarfed among a dozen or so big liveoak trees. The dark, crooked branches and their heavy year-around foliage shielded the structure from much of summer's hot afternoon sunshine and screened out some of winter's cold north wind. The house was probably as old as Wes himself, its roof divided into four equal quarters that came to a peak at the center. The windows were tall so summer's southern breezes could dispel heat otherwise trapped beneath the high ceilings. It had been seventy years since people had quit building houses in that style. Most ranches which had not torn them down by now were delegating them to transient help, mostly illegal Mexican aliens who paused to earn traveling money before moving northward in the hope of higher-paying big-city employment.

Beyond the house lay Wes's livestock-working corrals, a few of steel but most of aging lumber and cedar pickets, sadly showing their years. One, most ancient of all, was built of stones, stacked without mortar, a legacy from the hard labor of ambitious German immigrants who had braved their way into these resisting hills when this had still been Indian country. Almost everything he could see looked old. An exception was a steel barn Wes had put up after a high wind took part of the roof from his old one and set the rest of the tired structure to leaning eastward. Jim Ed remembered his father's anger. Truman Hendrix declared that Wes had let Grandmother Maudie live in that drafty old house for forty-odd years, but he had built a new barn for himself. The priorities of an old-fashioned, tight-twisted rancher were not easy to understand. . . .

Jim Ed and Wes stood on the porch, watching the dog trail Bill Roper's pickup the first fifty yards and then stood in the thin curtain of dust it raised climbing the hill. Jim Ed said, "Well, it looks like *everybody* around here's not mad at you."

Wes grunted. "*Everybody* ain't hopin' to make somethin' off the land that belongs to *me*."

That pie was probably more than Wes normally ate for supper, Jim Ed judged by the thin look of him. But Wes said, "We'll tend to the stock first, then fix supper. I reckon a growin' boy needs his nourishment."

"I'm not a boy," Jim Ed said, "and I'm done growing."

"Your Uncle James Edward never could seem to get enough to eat. He was always lookin' ahead to supper." An old pain came into Wes's eyes. His gaze went to the mantel, to a studio portrait of a young cowboy who had some of Wes Hendrix's features.

James Edward Hendrix. He had died before Jim Ed was born. Jim Ed had inherited his name.

Wes hobbled to the mantel and reached toward the photo but stopped short of touching it. "Everything I ever wanted was for James Edward and your daddy. All the time they was growin' up, I was gettin' this ranch ready for them. Your daddy never liked it, but James Edward did. Wasn't nothin' he couldn't do a-horseback. He could tell what a cow was fixin' to think before she thought it. Loved this place, that boy did."

He was silent a moment, then cleared his throat. "When you come along and they gave you his name, I sort of hoped that in a way you *were* him, come back to me. Remember when you was little? I let you ride in front of me on a horse."

Jim Ed remembered all too well. He had wet his britches out of fear that his grandfather would let him fall and the fool horse would step on him.

Wes went on, "You couldn't say *Granddad*, so you called me *Daddoo*. I kept hopin' your daddy might get tired of the city and move back to Big River. Then I could raise you to be the image of your uncle.

"But that's the way with dreams: the bad ones just haunt you, and the good ones never come true. People moved *away* from the country in them days; they didn't move *to* it."

When he turned from the picture, his eyes were more angry than sad. "Now it's in style for people to quit the city and move to the country, only they want to bring the city with them. Time they get through changin' it into everything they come here to run away from, there won't be nothin' left of the country."

Jim Ed said, "They'll pay you three times what this place is worth."

Wes's eyes crackled. "How do *you* know what it's worth? How do *you* put a price on forty-odd years? You ain't *lived* half that long.'' He stalked into the kitchen, where Jim Ed heard him running water into a tin bucket, rinsing it for the milking.

Jim Ed walked to the mantel and studied the picture of the uncle he knew only from a handful of old photographs. James Edward Hendrix could as well have lived a hundred years ago for all the closeness Jim Ed could feel toward him.

His attention shifted to another photograph, one much older and turning brown. It showed a slender young man on a pitching black horse, a rodeo crowd in the background. In fading ink near the bottom of the picture, he recognized his grandmother's hand: *Wes Hendrix, on Midnight.*

It seemed unreal, somehow, that Wes Hendrix had ever been that young. Had it not been for the writing, Jim Ed would not have recognized him.

Wes said gruffly, ''You better change into some old clothes, then meet me out at the barn. Even a city dude ought to learn how to feed stock and handle a milk cow. They'll pave over the last blade of grass someday, and drown the last tree in an artificial lake so some damnfool from town can race a motorboat. You ought to at least remember what it used to be like.''

Little had changed in his uncle's room in almost thirty years. Schoolbooks and a dozen Luke Short paperback Western novels still sat on a bookshelf, along with a silver trophy for exhibiting the county livestock show's grand champion steer in 1956, the last year of James Edward's life. Above the bookshelf hung a guitar probably not dusted since Maudie Hendrix died. Jim Ed examined a set of 45-rpm records in a box beside a big-spindle player. They carried such names as Hank Williams and Eddy Arnold, Gene Autry and Tex Ritter. Finding not even an

Elvis Presley, he closed the box and went out into the living room. His grandfather was slumped in a reclining chair that looked twice too large for him, reading the San Angelo *Standard-Times*.

Jim Ed asked, "What do you do around here for entertainment?"

Wes lowered the newspaper. "Entertainment?" It was as if he did not understand the word. "There's a whole shelf of good books yonder."

Jim Ed had already looked them over. A couple dealt with livestock health and nutrition. Most were on Texas and Western history, particularly about lawmen and outlaws and the ranching industry. Not one was on any subject Jim Ed considered relevant to the real world.

Wes said, "There's always the television."

It was a color set, probably Grandmother Maudie's choosing. Jim Ed turned it on but found only two stations. One resembled a January snowstorm. The other was showing an old movie he had already seen and didn't like.

Wes said, "Maudie always watched the soap operas. Them people was like old friends to her."

Jim Ed turned off the television. "How do you keep from going crazy out here all by yourself with nothing to do?"

Wes pondered. "A man can do worse than be by himself. He can read. He can think. He can sit on the porch and listen to the sounds of life out yonder."

Jim Ed argued, "There's nothing out there for miles."

"You just got to learn how to listen. It's all around you, like music."

Jim Ed frowned. His father was right. Wes Hendrix had been on this place too long for his own good.

Wes said, "James Edward knew. He was tuned to this place. He could tell you the name of everything that sang in the dark."

Jim Ed stood in the open front door, listening. He

heard only the high-pitched noise of crickets, the chatter of birds, the croaking of a frog down at a water tank, a cow bawling somewhere, the distant bleating of a lamb. He heard no music.

"We can't be somebody else," he commented. "I'm not James."

Wes's voice was so low Jim Ed barely heard it. "No, you sure as hell ain't." Wes got up and hunched out into the kitchen. He poured leftover coffee into a cup and fetched a bottle of bourbon out of the pantry. He poured a liberal amount of whisky into the coffee and extended the bottle toward Jim Ed. "You don't drink this stuff, do you?"

Before Jim Ed could say he did, Wes said he didn't. "You're too young. It can be balm to an *old* man, but it's a curse to a young one." He drank some of the coffee and refilled with pure whisky. Carrying the cup, he touched the wall switch and left the kitchen dark.

"Good night, Tater."

Jim Ed had trouble going to sleep. He dozed off, then awakened, momentarily disoriented. A gentle breeze from the south lifted the curtains around the open window. It was the noise that bothered him, or rather the lack of it. He heard no rumble of traffic, no horns, no television played too loudly.

Or perhaps he did. There *was* a sound of some kind, distant music that reached him in fragments torn by the breeze. He thought for a moment it was imagination, but he heard it again. He wondered if Wes might have left his bedroom radio playing softly when he went to sleep. Then he decided the sound came from outside. He slid out of bed and went to the window. He heard it more clearly, though it came from the other side of the house. He walked through the living room and out onto the porch.

He saw his grandfather's slight figure silhouetted against the moonlit barn, the dog beside him. Wes Hendrix sat on a bench under one of the huge liveoak trees, fiddle beneath his chin. He played a slow, melancholy melody, vaguely familiar though Jim Ed did not know its name.

He had not seen his grandfather weep at the funeral of Maudie Hendrix, and he had wondered how the old man could maintain such unyielding self-control. He sensed that Wes was weeping now, through the music he drew from that old fiddle.

Jim Ed listened until he began to feel uneasily that he was intruding on private grief. He quietly retreated into the house and returned to his bed. The last he knew as he dropped off to sleep, that music still reached him through the open window like a faraway cry for help that he did not know how to answer.